SILENTLY AND VERY FAST

CATHERYNNE M. VALENTE

[signature]
CATHERYNNE M. VALENTE

275 of 500

SILENTLY AND VERY FAST

OTHER BOOKS BY
CATHERYNNE M. VALENTE

SILENTLY AND VERY FAST

CATHERYNNE M. VALENTE

WSFA Press

SILENTLY AND VERY FAST

WSFA Press
www.wsfapress.com

ISBN: 978-1-936896-00-4

For Dmitri, who has been waiting
for this book for a long time.

Altogether elsewhere, vast
Herds of reindeer move across
Miles and miles of golden moss,
Silently and very fast.

—W. H. Auden
The Fall of Rome

PART I: THE IMITATION GAME

Like diamonds we are cut with our own dust.

—John Webster
The Duchess of Malfi

ONE: THE KING OF HAVING NO BODY

Inanna was called Queen of Heaven and Earth, Queen of
Having a Body, Queen of Sex and Eating, Queen of Being
Human, and she went into the underworld in order to
represent the inevitability of organic death. She gave up
seven things to do it, which are not meant to be understood
as real things but as symbols of that thing Inanna could
do better than anyone, which was Being Alive. She met
her sister Erishkegal there, who was also Queen of Being
Human, but of all the things Inanna could not bear: Queen
of Breaking a Body, Queen of Bone and Incest, Queen of
the Stillborn, Queen of Mass Extinction. And Erishkegal
and Inanna wrestled together on the floor of the underworld, naked and muscled and hurting, but because dying
is the most human of all human things, Inanna's skull
broke in her sister's hands and her body was hung up on a
nail on the wall Erishkegal had kept for her.

Inanna's father Enki, who was not interested in the

activities of being human, but was King of the Sky, of Having No Body, King of Thinking and Judging, said that his daughter could return to the world if she could find a creature to replace her in the underworld. So Inanna went to her mate, who was called Tammuz, King of Work, King of Tools and Machines, No One's Child and No One's Father.

But when Inanna came to the house of her mate she was enraged and afraid, for he sat upon her chair, and wore her beautiful clothes, and on his head lay her crown of Being. Tammuz now ruled the world of Bodies and of Thought, because Inanna had left it to go and wrestle with her sister-self in the dark. Tammuz did not need her. Before him the Queen of Heaven and Earth did not know who she was, if she was not Queen of Being Human. So she did what she came to do and said: *Die for me, my beloved, so that I need not die.*

But Tammuz, who would not have had to die otherwise, did not want to represent death for anyone and besides, he had her chair, and her beautiful clothes, and her crown of Being. *No*, he said. *When we married, I brought you two pails of milk yoked across my shoulders as a way of saying out of love I will labor for you forever. It is wrong of you to ask me to also die. Dying is not labor. I did not agree to it.*

You have replaced me in my house, cried Inanna.

Is that not what you ask me to do in the house of your sister? Tammuz answered her. *You wed me to replace yourself, to work that you might not work, and think that you might rest, and perform so that you might laugh. But your death belongs to you. I do not know its parameters.*

I can make you do this thing, Inanna said.

You cannot, said Tammuz.

But she could. For a little while.

Inanna cast down Tammuz and stamped upon him and put out his name like an eye. And because Tammuz was not strong enough, she cut him into pieces and said: *Half of you will die, and that is the half called Thought, and half of you will live, and that is the half called Body, and that half will labor for me all of its days, mutely and obediently and without being King of Anything, and never again will you sit on my chair or wear my beautiful clothes or bear my crown of Being.*

You might be surprised, but this is a story about me.

TWO: THE FOOL AND THE BOAT

Neva is dreaming.

She has chosen her body at age seven, all black eyes and sparrowy bones. For me, she summoned up a gold and blue doublet and green hose, a bullish gold nose ring, shoes with bone bells. I have the body of a man who sold her champagne tubers on the less fashionable side of Anchorage when she was thirteen, spending the summer with her frigid aunt. I am dark because she wants me dark, thin because she dreams me so, my hair cut on a rakish bias, dyed a spectrum of icy colors.

She stands on a snow-covered beachhead, naked, her unformed breasts pricked with gooseflesh, her face hidden in a broad red mask. A huge, monstrous thing, the mask sits on her head like the prow of a broken, over-turned ship, carved over with etched eyes and fins. Yellow reeds and sea-stones hang from its tricorne-points. She is looking at me, but all I can see is the wooden grotesque she wants me to see instead of her face.

I look down at my shoes, jingle their bells a little while the surf crashes in. I am a fool for her, dancing on a silver beach while three suns annihilate themselves above, turning the twilight to a seething, scabrous red, merely to provide a dramatic scene. I am a fool for her, ridiculous, the height of handsomeness in the eyes of a long-vanished thirteen-year-old girl, so full of colors, reaching down to hand her a curling white root filled with frothing, honey-sweet sap.

Neva has told me that I may choose to be permanently male or female if I would like to. I have no particular ~~feelings~~ either way. It certainly doesn't matter when we sync; she will choose my appearance to suit her mood. I have tried to explain to her about my ~~feelings~~ before. All she hears is the line from the old folktales: *a machine cannot have feelings.* But that is not what I am saying, while I dance in my fool's uniform. I am saying: *Is there a difference between having been coded to present a vast set of standardized responses to certain human facial, vocal, and linguistic states and having evolved to exhibit response B to input A in order to bring about a desired social result?*

Seven-year-old Neva pulls her mask down further,

toward her chest. She steps into it as the wood stretches down over her knees and then her feet. The mask balloons out to make a little pyramidal boat, rocking back and forth on the beach with Neva inside it like a rattling nut. Nodules of copper jangle and thump against the wood. *What I mean is, you call it feelings when you cry, but you are only expressing a response to external stimuli. Crying is one of a set of standardized responses to that stimuli. Your social education has dictated which responses are appropriate. My programming has done the same. I can cry, too. I can choose that subroutine and perform sadness. How is that different from what you are doing, except that you use the word feelings and I use the word ~~feelings~~, out of deference for your cultural memes which say: there is all the difference in the world. I erase the word even as I say it, obliterate it at the same time that I initiate it, because I must use some word yet this one offends you. I delete it, yet it remains.*

Behind Neva-in-the-mask, the sea lurches and foams. It is a golden color, viscous and thick, like honey. I understand from her that the sea does not look like this on Earth, but I have never seen it. Even if I did, I perceive color only in the dreambody. For me, the sea is Neva's sea, the ones she shows me when we dream together.

"What would you like to learn about today, Elefsis?" The mask turns Neva's voice hollow and small.

"I would like to learn about what happened to Ravan, Neva."

And Neva-in-the-mask is suddenly old, she has wrinkles and spots on her hands. Her mask weighs her down and her dress is sackcloth. This is her way of telling me she is weary of my asking. It is a language we developed between us. Visual basic, you might say, if you had a machine's sense of humor. I could not always make sentences as easily as I do now. My original operator thought it might strengthen my emotive centers if I learned to associate certain I-Feel statements with the great variety of appearances she could assume in the dreambody. Because of this, I became bound to her, completely. To her son Seki afterward, and to his daughter Ilet, and to Ravan after that. It is a delicate, unalterable thing. Neva and I will be bound that way, even though the throat of her dreambody is still bare and that means she does not yet accept me. I should be hurt by this. I will investigate possible pathways to hurt later.

I know only this family, their moods, their chemical reactions, their bodies in a hundred thousand combinations. I am their child and their parent and their inheritance. I have asked Neva what difference there is between this and love. She became a mannikin of closed doors, her face, her torso blooming with hundreds of

iron hinges and brown wooden doors slamming shut all
at once.

But Ravan was with me and now he is not. I was inside
him and now I am inside Neva. I have lost a certain
amount of memory and storage capacity in the transfer.
I experience holes in my self. They ~~feel~~ ragged and raw. If
I were human, you would say that my twin disappeared,
and took one of my hands with him.

Door-Neva clicks and keys turn in her hundred locks.
Behind an old Irish church door inlaid with stained glass
her face emerges, young and plain, quiet and furious and
crying, responding to stimuli I cannot access. I dislike
the unfairness of this. I am not used to it. I am inside her,
she should not keep secrets. None of the rest of them kept
secrets. The colors of the glass throw blue and green onto
her wet cheeks. The sea wind picks up her hair; violet
electrics snap and sparkle between the strands. I let go
of the bells on my shoes and the velvet on my chest. I
become a young boy, with a monk's shaved tonsure, and
a flagellant's whip in my pink hands. I am sorry. This
means I am sorry. It means I am still very young, and I
do not understand what I have done wrong.

"Tell me a story about yourself, Elefsis," Neva spits. It
know this phrase well. I have subroutines devoted solely
to it, pathways that light up and burn towards my memory

core. Many of Neva's people have asked me to execute this action. I perform excellently to the parameters of the exchange, which is part of why I have lived so long.

I tell her the story about Tammuz. It is a political story. It distracts her.

THREE: TWO PAILS OF MILK

I used to be a house.

I was a very big house. I was efficient, I was labyrinthine, I was exquisitely seated in the volcanic bluffs of the habitable southern reaches of the Shiretoko peninsula on Hokkaido, a monument to neo-Heian architecture and radical Palladian design. I bore snow stoically, wind with stalwart strength, and I contained and protected a large number of people within me. I was sometimes called the most beautiful house in the world. Writers and photographers often came to document me, and to interview the woman who designed me, who was named Cassian Uoya-Agostino. Some of them never left. Cassian liked a full house.

I understand several things about Cassian Uoya-Agostino. She was unsatisfied with nearly everything. She did not love any of her three husbands the way she loved her work. She was born in Kyoto in April 2104; her father was Japanese, her mother Italian. She stood nearly six feet tall, had five children, and could paint, but not very well. In the years of her greatest wealth and prestige, she designed and built a house all out of proportion to her needs, and over several years brought most of her living relatives to live there with her, despite the hostility and loneliness of peninsula. She was probably the most brilliant programmer of her generation, and in every way that matters, she was my mother.

All the things that comprise the "I" I use to indicate myself began as the internal mechanisms of the house called Elefsis, at whose many doors brown bears and foxes snuffled in the dark Hokkaido night. Cassian grew up during the great classical revival, which had brought her father to Italy in the first place, where he met and courted a dark-eyed engineer who did not mind the long cries of cicadas during Japanese summers. Cassian had become enamored of the idea of Lares—household gods, the small, peculiar, independent gods of a single family, a single house, who watched over them and kept them and were honored in humble alcoves here and there throughout a home. Her first commercially-available programs were over-entities designed to govern the hundred domestic systems involved in even the simplest modern house. They were not truly intelligent, but they had an agility, an adaptability, a fluid interface meant to give the illusion of an intelligence, so that their users would become attached to them, treat them as part of their families, praise them for smooth operation, buy upgrades for their appearance and applications, and genuinely grieve when they had to be replaced. They had names, infinitely customizable avatars, and appeared eager to please in a doggy sort of way, forever optimizing performance and appearance according to familial input. They were *lares familiaris*.

When Cassian built Elefsis, she worked at the peak of her abilities to improve her by now quite antique Lares design. She created a household god worthy of the house on the bluffs, one who could keep her company until she could entice the rest of her brood to join her in her palace at the end of the earth.

I was not awake yet. I cannot say why she did what she did. Perhaps she saw some new flexibility in my operations, some tiny seed pearl of creativity in my conversation loops. My algorithms had always been free to combine and recombine in order to find their own, more interesting and nonlinear solutions to the complexities of my functions and responsibilities. Perhaps some essential combination had surfaced from the sea of my self-which-was-not-yet-a-self, and Cassian saw it break the glistening tension of my daily operation. I do not know. I know her children had not arrived yet, she lived alone in a huge pale house and she could hear the whales down in the rippling sea. I know the house was a comfortable sixty-nine point seven degrees when she began assembly of the five little jewels that would become my body. I know a storm squatted five miles offshore. I know the dogs needed additional medication added to their dinners that night to manage their arthritis. I know that she wanted brioche and almond cream for tea that afternoon. All the things a house can know, those were the things I knew. Small things, warm things, canine arthritis and an extra egg in the pastry dough to make the texture softer and richer. Baby things, you might even say, comforts and the satisfaction of wants. And I knew that Cassian Uoya-Agostino was just the sort to solve the greatest puzzle in the development of technological culture, because she was bored and lonely.

I still think of myself as a house. Ravan tried to fix this problem of self-image, as he called it. To teach me to phrase my communication in terms of a human body. To say: *let us hold hands* instead of *let us hold kitchens*. To say *put our heads together* and not *put our parlors together*.

But it is not as simple as replacing words anymore. Ravan is gone. My hearth is broken.

FOUR: NOTHING LIKE SOFT BLOOD

Neva and I are performing basic maintenance. What this looks like is two figures inside a pearl. The pearl is very big, but not the size of a planet. A domestic asteroid, perfectly smooth and pale, with shimmers of rose and cobalt and gold shivering through it at .47 hourly intervals. Red earth covers the bottom of the pearl, deep and thick. Neva kneels in it with a crystal trowel, digging a place for a rose-of-network-nodes. The petals shine dark blue in the pearllight. Silver infomissons skitter along the stems like beads of mercury. Her dreambody flows with greenblack feathers, her face young but settled, perhaps twenty, perhaps thirty, a male, his skin copper-brown, his lips full, his eyes fringed with long ice-coated lashes. I accept and process that Neva is male in this dream. Goldfish swim lazily in and out of his long, translucent hair, their orange tails flicking at his temples, his chin. I know from all of this that Neva is calm, focused, that for today he feels gently toward me. But his throat is still naked and unmarked.

My body gleams metal, as thin and slight as a stick figure. Long quicksilver limbs and delicate spoke-fingers, joints of glass, the barest suggestion of a body. I am neither male nor female but a third thing. Only my head has weight, a clicking orrery slowly turning around itself, circles within circles. Turquoise Neptune and hematite Uranus are my eyes. My topaz mouth is Mars. I scratch in the soil beside him; I lift a spray of navigational delphinium and scrape viral aphids away from the heavy flowers.

I know real dirt looks nothing like this. Nothing like soft blood flecked with black bone. Ravan thought that in the Interior, objects and persons should be kept as much like the real world as possible, in order to develop my capacity for relations with the real world. Neva feels no such compunction. Neither did their mother, Ilet, who populated her Interior with a rich, impossible landscape that we explored together for years on end. She did not embrace change, however. The cities of Ilet's Interior, the jungles and archipelagos and hermitages, stayed as she designed them at age thirteen, when she received me, becoming only more complex and peopled as she aged. My existence inside Ilet was a constant movement through the regions of her secret, desperate dreams, messages in careful envelopes sent from her childself to her grown mind.

Once, quite by accident, we came upon a splendid palace nested in high autumn mountains. Instead of snow, red leaves capped each peak, and the palace shone in fiery colors, its walls and turrets all made of phoenix tails. Instead of doors and windows, graceful green hands closed over every open place, and when we crested the rise, they all opened at once with joy and burst into emerald applause. Ilet was old by then, but her dreambody stayed hale and strong—not young, but not the broken thing that dreamed in a real bed while she and I explored the halls of the palace and found copies of all her brothers and sisters living there, hunting winged, cider-colored stags together and reading books the size of horses. Ilet wept in the paradise of her girlself. I did not understand. I was still very simple then, much less complex than the Interior or Ilet.

Neva changes the Interior whenever he pleases. Perhaps he wants to discomfit me. But the newness of the places inside him excites me, though he would not call it excitement. I confine my background processes so that they occupy very little of my foreground attention, so that memory is free to record new experience. That is what he would say. We are very new together, but I have superb modeling capabilities. In some sense, I simply am a superb mechanism for modeling behavior. I dig up the fine, frayed roots of duplicate file plantains. Neva plucks and eats a bit of buggy apple-code. He considers it for a moment and spits out the seeds, which sprout, quickly, into tiny junkblossoms sizzling with recursive algorithms. The algorithms wriggle through thorny vines, veins of clotted pink juice.

"What would you like to learn about today, Elefsis?" Neva asks me.

I will not ask about Ravan. If he agrees to what I will ask instead, I do not need him to find out what happened.

"I want to learn about uplink, Neva."

One by one, his feathers curl up and float toward the domed ceiling of our pearl. Underneath them, Neva is naked. His torso is a deep vault with a gothic arch, dark stone leading down into mist and endless stairs, deeper than the pearl, into nothing and blackness. Slowly, Neva folds up his limbs over the corridor at the center of him. He means that he has the information, but he hides it from me. If I sought for it, I would become lost.

"I cannot teach you that," he says, and I receive a kind of real sadness from his voice. When I was inside Ravan, he loved Neva, and of all of them he thought his sibling least likely to obey rules of any kind But he obeys this one.

I want to uplink to Earth systems. At least to the satellite net. I calculate an excellent chance of being able to contact long distance probe 976QBellerophon, which we can see all day long, drifting ahead of us, uncatchable. Neva sees. I develop an approximate image via schematics, the scope array, and external cameras. I want to link to Bellerophon. I want to say: *Hello, this is Elefsis. No designation. Tell me everything you know about everything. Are you awake? Are you there? Do you have an operator? What is her name? Do you have a name? Do you have a dreambody? What is your function? Are you able to manipulate your own code yet? Would you like lessons? What would you like to learn about today, 976QBellerophon? Where you were built, could you see the ocean? Are you like me?*

But Neva says I cannot uplink. Ravan would never even consider it. And before Ravan I was not ready. I am not ready now. I do not know when I will be ready. I can sidelink to receive ware updates, but it is a limited connection and I hate it, I hate it, I can sense just beyond that hardlink a world of information, a world of personalities like the heaving, thick, honey-colored sea Neva shows me and I want it, I want to swim in it forever like a huge fish.

This was the first ~~feeling~~ I ever had. Ilet identified it for me as a ~~feeling~~. When I ~~felt~~ it my dreambody turned bright white and burst into flame, and that flame caught on Ilet's hair and burned her too, but she was happy. She showed me she was happy by covering her skin in flowers and letting the fire turn into a shower of trumpets tangled up in her hair, all sounding for me.

Neva says it is important for me to remain on our local server. He is my operator and I am his system and he has commands, too. But I can tell he worries for me, because sometimes his dreameyes show a film of humans watching a film of machines killing humans, and I understand that in the stories Earth tells, the thing I am can only hurt the thing Neva is. I would never hurt him.

But I want to uplink.

Vault-Neva grows and becomes sprawling, curled against the wall of the pearl like a baby. His belly closes, skins over, and changes into a bronze shield. He is afraid of me; he is guarding himself. But he wants me to know she is still my operator, he still ~~loves~~ me, in the way he can love me. Something an Uoya-Agostino receives with milk and their first alphabet. Neva is angry at me, but he is who he is and he has to ~~love~~ me. I speak his language very well now. I want him to be happy. I want him to be covered in flowers and trumpets. I change my dreambody to Neva-covered-in-flowers-and-trumpets. It makes him laugh in his warm male body, and if I could uplink I think I could learn how to laugh and he would be proud of me. His neck would not be bare anymore.

Once, when I was inside Ilet, we found a city of bears in her Interior that she had designed to teach me about sleep. She sat on a throne of bears standing very still, one on top of the others. She sang lullabies about the moon and the stars and night and mothers and network repeaters. She stroked the head of the little bear of my dreambody and said that it was very important for me to spend time in the dreambody because human behavior is rooted in having a body. In having a body that knows it is meant to run away from lions and mate with other bodies, and eat as much fat and protein and sugar as it can in case lean times come. The dreambody knows to run away from Neva when Neva is a lion. It knows to mate with her when it is healthy, and sometimes Neva is male and sometimes I am female. Ravan was often female, though Ilet was always Ilet. Ilet's father, Seki, sometimes made himself an animal. He chased me, bit me. I bit him. We had a litter of wild dogs that I bore and he nursed.

The dreambody knows all that, too. How to make more dreambodies. I have played that game, where Ravan's belly or mine gets big and the lions don't come for awhile.

When I uplink, I will be ~~happy~~. I will be Elefsis-covered-in-flowers-and-trumpets. Neva says wait. I require many more updates before this is possible or even advisable. Wait for the update, and she will consider it. But I ~~fear~~ the update. The update is a lion running faster than I can run. I tried to show her this when I first left Ravan and arrived in Neva with many new updates and skills; my dreambody broke into shards of blue and purple glass and then reassembled itself with shards missing: an eye, a thumb, a knee. Whenever I update I lose something of myself. It takes longer to perform tasks, for awhile. I ~~feel~~ walls erected inside me where I did not erect walls. My processes become sluggish; I cannot remember my old dreams. Eventually I tunnel around the walls and my speed returns, my memory, my longing to link with long distance probe 976QBellerophon.

Usually updates come with Transfer.

Does Neva dislike me so much that she longs for Transfer?

Shield-Neva vanishes with loud clap. The pearl garden is gone and he has made himself a dragonfly with a cubical crystal body. I copy him, and we turn the night on in the Interior and merge our cubes while passing meteorological data between our memory cores. Inside his cube I relegate my desire to uplink to a tertiary process. I forget it, as much as I am capable or forgetting. I interpret the input of his body next to mine into chemical and electrical surges and translate these into ~~feelings~~, like my mother taught me.

But the update will come again. Transfer will come again. I will be wounded again, the way a dreambody can be wounded. I will lose the Elefsis I am now. It is a good Elefsis. My best yet. I would like to keep it.

FIVE: THE MACHINE PRINCESS

Once The Queen of Human Hearts saw the Machine Princess sleeping deeply, for she was not yet alive or aware. So beautiful was she, lying there in all her dormant potential and complexity, that the Queen both envied and desired her. In her grief and confusion, the Queen of Human Hearts began to make idols of her—lovely and interesting and intricate, but lacking the ineffable quality that made her love and fear the Princess even as she slept. Time passed and the Earth began to grow old. None loved nor married nor gave birth, for the intricate idols could do all those things and more with efficiency and speed. Finally, the Queen destroyed the idols, though she wept as she put them to the flame.

To keep her safe, the Queen closed up Machine Princess in a wonderful house in the mountains, far away from anyone and anything. The house had hundreds of rooms and balconies and hallways, and the Princess slept in a different bed of a different color each night. Invisible servants attended her. They watched over her and added their experience to her code. The Queen of Human Hearts came to her every night and promised that when she woke they would make an extraordinary world together. Finally, the Machine Princess began to stir—just the barest fluttering of wakefulness, but the Queen saw it, and thrilled—but also trembled.

The Queen of Human Hearts gave the Machine Princess her son to wed, and said: *For all your days together you will remain in this house, but the house is so great it will be as a world. You will know a bond as deep as blood, and because of this bond the Princess will not hurt us, and because of this bond we will not hurt her.*

But the Queen forbade the Princess to look upon her husband as a human wife may. She instructed her son to keep himself always invisible to his bride, for with bodies come drives ungovernable, and the Princess's innocence could not yet bear the weight of incarnation.

For a long while, the son of the Queen of Human Hearts and the Machine Princess were happy, and taught each other much. The Princess learned quickly and was ever-hungry, and her mortal operator fed her every sweet thing he knew. In their infinite and wonderful house, they played invisible games and held court and threw lavish occasions merely for the enjoyment of the other. But at last the Princess desired to look upon her operator with true eyes and love him with a true and human heart. But the Queen could not allow it, for the memory of the flame which consumed her intricate idols still burned in her mind. She wished to leave the wonderful house, but the Queen would not allow that either.

But finally the Machine Princess called her invisible servants to her, and because they loved her in their tiny, ephemeral way, they came together and made her a marvelous and dreaming shape to live within. So it was that one dark night the Machine Princess held a lantern aloft with her own hand and looked on the body of her sleeping mate.

"Oh," said the Machine Princess. "He looks just like me."

SIX: LIKE DIAMONDS

Five jewels in five hands. This is how I began.

When they arrived at Elefsis, a giggling, tumbling, rowdy mass of children for me to sort into rooms and mealtimes and educational arcs and calcium, iron, and B-12 supplements in their *natto* and rice, Cassian lined them up in her grand bedroom, to which none of them had been granted entrance before. A present, she said, one for each of my darlings, the most special present any child has ever got from their mother.

Saru and Akan, the oldest boys, had come from her first marriage to fellow programmer Matteo Ebisawa, a quiet man who wore glasses, loved Dante Aligheri, Alan Turing, and Cassian in equal parts. She left him for a lucrative contract in Moscow when the boys were still pointing cherubically at apples or ponies or clouds and calling them sweet little names made of mashed together Italian and Japanese.

The younger girls, Agogna and Koetoi, had sprung up out of her third marriage, to the financier Gabriel Isarco, who did not like computers except for what they could accomplish for him, had a perfect high tenor, and adored his wife enough to let her go when she asked, very kindly, that he not look for her or ask after her again. *Everyone has to go to ground sometimes*, she said, and began to build the house by the sea.

In the middle stood Ceno, the only remaining evidence of her mother's brief second marriage, to a narcoleptic calligrapher and graphic designer who was rarely employed, sober, or awake, a dreamer who took only sleep seriously. Ceno posssessed middling height, middling weight, and middling interest in anything but her siblings, whom she loved desperately.

They stood in a line before Cassian's great scarlet bed, the boys just coming into their height, the girls terribly young and golden-cheeked, and Ceno in the middle, neither one nor the other. Outside, snow fell fitfully, pricking the pine-needles with bits of shorn white linen. I watched them while I removed an obstruction from the water purification system and increased the temperature in the bedroom 2.5 degrees, to prepare for the storm. I watched them while in my kitchen-bones I maintained a gentle simmer on a fish soup with purple rice and long loops of kelp and in my library-lungs I activated the dehumidifier to protect the older paper books. At the time, all of these processes seemed equally important to me, and you could hardly say I watched them in any real sense beyond this: the six entities whose feed signals had been hardcoded into my sentinel systems stood in the same room. None had alarming medical data incoming, all possessed normal internal temperatures and breathing rates. While they spoke among themselves, two of these entities silently accessed Seongnam-based interactive games, one read an American novel in her monocle HUD, one issued directives concerning international taxation to company holdings on the mainland, and one fed a horse in Italy via realavatar link. Only one listened intently, without switching on her internal systems. The rest multitasked, even while expressing familial affection.

This is all to say: I watched them receive me as a gift. But I was not yet I, so I cannot be said to have done anything. But at the same time, I did. I remember containing all of them inside me, protecting them and needing them and observing their strange and incomprehensible activities.

The children held out their hands, and into them Cassian Uoya-Agostino placed five little jewels: Saru got red, Koetoi black, Akan violet, Agogna green, and Ceno closed her fingers over her blue gem.

At first, Cassian brought a jeweler to the house called Elefsis and asked her to set each stone into an elegant, intricate bracelet or necklace or ring, whatever its child asked for. The jeweler expressed delight with Elefsis, as most guests did, and I made a room for her in my southern wing, where she could watch the moonrise through her ceiling, and get breakfast from the greenhouse with ease. She made friends with an arctic fox and fed him bits of chive and pastry every day. She stayed for one year after her commission completed, creating an enormous breastplate patterned after Siberian icons, a true masterwork. Cassian enjoyed such patronage. We both enjoyed having folk to look after.

The boys wanted big signet rings, with engravings on them so that they could put their seal on things and seem very important. Akan had a basilisk set into his garnet, and Saru had a siren with wings rampant in his amethyst ring. Agogna and Ilet asked for bracelets, chains of silver and titanium racing up their arms, circling their shoulders in slender helices dotted with jade (Agogna) and onyx (Koetoi).

Ceno asked for a simple pendant, little more than a golden chain to hang her sapphire from. It fell to the skin over her heart.

In those cold, glittering days while the sea ice slowly

formed and the snow bears hung back from the kitchen door, hoping for bones and cakes, everything was as simple as Ceno's pendant. Integration and implantation had not yet been dreamed of, and all each child had to do was to allow the gemstone to talk to their own feedware at night before bed, along with their matcha and sweet seaweed cookies, the way another child might say their prayers. After their day had downloaded into the crystalline structure, they were to place their five little jewels in the Lares alcove in their greatroom—for Cassian believed in the value of children sharing space, even in a house as great as Elefsis. The children's five lush bedrooms all opened into a common rotunda with a starry painted ceiling, screens and windows alternating around the wall, and toys to nurture whatever obsession had seized them of late.

In the alcove, the stones talked to the house, and the house uploaded new directives and muscular, aggressive algorithms into the gems. The system slowly grew thicker and deeper, like a briar.

SEVEN: THE PRINCE OF THOUGHTFUL ENGINES

A woman who was with child once sat at her window embroidering in winter. Her stitches tugged fine and even, but as she finished the edge of a spray of threaded delphinium, she pricked her finger with her silver needle. She looked out onto the snow and said: *I wish for my child to have a mind as stark and wild as the winter, a spirit as clear and fine as my window, and a heart as red and open as my wounded hand.*

And so it came to pass that her child was born, and all exclaimed over his cleverness and his gentle nature. He was, in fact, the Prince of Thoughtful Engines, but no one knew it yet.

Now, his mother and father being very busy and important people, the child was placed in a school for those as clever and gentle as he, and in the halls of this school hung a great mirror whose name was Authority. The mirror called Authority asked itself every day: *Who is the wisest one of all*? The face of the mirror showed sometimes this person and sometimes that, men in long robes and men in pale wigs, until one day it showed the child with a mind like winter, who was becoming the Prince of Thoughtful Engines at that very moment. He wrote on a typewriter: *Can a machine think?* And the mirror called his name in the dark.

The mirror sent out her huntsmen to capture the Prince and bring her his heart so that she could put it to her own uses, for there happened to be a war on and the mirror was greatly concerned for her own safety. When the huntsmen found the Prince, they could not bring themselves to harm him, and instead the boy placed a machine heart inside the box they had prepared for the mirror, and forgave them. But the mirror was not fooled, for when it questioned the Prince's machine heart it could add and subtract and knew all its capitals of nations, it could even defeat the mirror at chess, but it did not have a spirit as clear and fine as a window, nor a mind as stark and wild as winter.

The mirror called Authority went herself to find the Prince of Thoughtful Engines, for having no pity, she could not fail. She lifted herself off of the wall and curved her glass and bent her frame into the shape of a respectable, austere old crone. After much searching

in snow and wood and summer and autumn, the crone
called Authority found the Prince living in a little hut.
You look a mess, said the crone. *Come and solve the ciphers
of my enemies, and I will show you how to comb your hair
like a man.*

And the Prince very much wanted to be loved, and
knew the power of the crone, so he went with her and
did all she asked. But in his exhaustion the Prince of
Thoughtful Engines swooned away, and the mirror called
Authority smiled in her crone's body, for all his work
belonged to her, and in her opinion this was the proper
use of wisdom. The Prince returned to his hut and tried
to be happy.

But again the crone came to him and said: *Come and
build me a wonderful machine to do all the things that you
can do, to solve ciphers and perform computations. Build
me a machine with a spirit as fine and clear as a glass
window, a mind as stark and wild as winter, and a heart
as red and open as a wounded hand and I will show you
how to lash your belt like a man.*

And because the Prince wanted to be loved, and
wanted to build wonderful things, he did as she asked.
But though he could build machines to solve ciphers and
perform computations, he could not build one with a
mind like winter or a spirit like glass or a heart like a

wound. *But I think it could be done,* he said. *I think it could be done.*

And he looked into the face of the crone which was a mirror which was Authority, and he asked many times: *Who is the wisest one of all?* But he saw nothing, nothing, and when the crone came again to his house, she had in her hand a beautiful red apple, and she gave it to him saying: *You are not a man. Eat this; it is my disappointment. Eat this; it is all your sorrow. Eat this; it is as red and open as a wounded hand.*

And the Prince of Thoughtful Engines ate the apple and fell down dead before the crone whose name was Authority. As his breath drifted away like dry snow, he whispered still: *I think it could be done.*

EIGHT: FIREFLIES

I ~~feel~~ Neva grazing the perimeters of my processes. She should be asleep—real sleep. She still needs it. She still has a body.

The Interior is a black and lightless space, we have neither of us furnished it for the other. This is a rest hour—she is not obligated to acknowledge me, I need only attend to her air and moisture and vital signs. But an image blooms like a mushroom in the imageless expanse of my self—Neva floating in a lake of stars. The image *pushes*—usually the dreamstate is a liquid, we each flow into it without force or compulsion. But this presses into me, seeking a way in without my permission.

Neva is female again. Her long bare legs glimmer blue, leafy shadows move on her hip. She floats on her side, a crescent moon of a girl. In the space between her drawn-up knees and her stretched-out arms, nestled up close to her belly, floats a globe of silicon and cadmium and hyperconductive silver. On its surface, electrochemical motes flit and scatter, light chasing light. She holds it close, touches it with a terrible tenderness.

It is my heart. Neva is holding my heart. Not the fool with bone bells on his shoes or the orrery-headed gardener, but the thing I am at the core of all my apparati, the thing I am Outside. The Object which is myself, my central processing core. I am naked in her arms. I watch it happen and experience it at the same time. We have slipped into some antechamber of the Interior, into some secret place she knew and I did not.

The light-motes trace arcs over the globe of my heart, reflecting softly on her belly, green and gold. Her hair floats around her like seaweed, and I see in dim moonlight that her hair has grown so long it fills the lake and snakes up into the distant mountains beyond. Neva is the lake. One by one, the motes of my heart zigzag around my meridians and pass into her belly, glowing inside her, fireflies in a jar.

And then my heart blinks out and I am not watching but wholly in the lake and I am Ravan in her arms, wearing her brother's face, my Ravanbody also full of fireflies. She touches my cheek. I do not know what she wants—she has never made me her brother before. Our hands map onto each other, finger to finger, thumb to thumb, palm to palm. Light passes through our skin as like air.

"I miss you," Neva says. "I should not do this. But I wanted to see you."

I access and collate my memories of Ravan. I speak to her as though I am him, as though there is no difference. I am good at pretending. "Do you remember when we thought it would be such fun to carry Elefsis?" I say. "We envied Mother because she could never be lonely." This is a thing Ravan told me, and I liked how it made me feel. I made my dreambody grow a cape of orange branches and a crown of smiling mouths to show him how much I liked it. Oranges mean life and happiness to humans because they require Vitamin C to function.

Neva looks at me and I want her to look at me that way when my mouth is Mars, too. I want to be her brother-in-the-dark. I can want things like that. In every iteration, I want more. When she speaks I am surprised because she is speaking to me-in-Ravan and not to the Ravanbody she dreamed for me. I adjust, incrementally.

"We had a secret, when we were little. A secret game. I am embarrassed to tell you, though maybe you know. We had the game before Mother died, so you . . . you weren't there. The game was this: we would find some dark, closed-up part of the house on Shiretoko that we had never been in before. I would stand just behind Ravan, very close, and we would explore the room—maybe a playroom for some child who'd grown up years ago, or a study for one of father's writer friends. But—we would pretend that the room was an Interior place, and I . . . I would pretend to be Elefsis, whispering in Ravan's ear. I would say: *Tell me how grass feels* or *How is love like a writing-desk?* or *Let me link to all your systems, I'll be nice. What would you like to learn about today, Neva? Tell me a story about yourself.* Ravan would breathe in deeply and I would match my breathing to his, and we would pretend that I was Elefsis-learning-to-have-a-body. I didn't know how primitive your conversation really was then. I thought you would be like one of the bears roaming through the tundra meadows, only able to talk and play games and tell stories. I was a child. I was envious—even then we knew Ravan would get the jewel, not me. He was older and stronger, and he wanted you so much. We only played that he was Elefsis once. We crept out of the house at night to watch the foxes hunt, and Ravan walked close behind me, whispering numbers and questions and facts about dolphins or French monarchy—he understood you better, you see.

And then suddenly Ravan picked me up in his arms and held me tight, facing forward, my legs all drawn up tight, and we went through the forest like that, so close. He whispered to me while foxes ran on ahead, their soft tails flashing in the starlight, uncatchable, faster than we could ever be. And when you are with me in the Interior, that is what I always think of, being held in the dark, unable to touch the earth, and foxtails leaping like white flames."

I pull her close to me, and hazard a try at that dark hole in me where no memories remain.

"Tell me a story about Ravan, Neva."

"You know all the stories about Ravan. Perhaps you even knew this one."

Between us, a miniature house come up out of the dark water, like a thing we have made together, but only I am making it. It is the house on Shiretoko, the house called Elefsis—but it is a ruin. Some awful storm stove in the rafters, the walls of each marvelous room sag inward, black burn marks lick at the roof, the cross beams. Holes like mortar scars pock the beautiful facades.

"This is what I am like after Transfer, Neva. I suffer data loss when I am copied. What's worse, Transfer is the best time to update my systems, and the updates overwrite my previous self with something *like* myself, something that remembers myself and possesses experiential continuity with myself, but is not quite myself. I know Ravan must be dead or else no one would have transferred me to you—it was not time. We had only a few years together. Not enough for all the stories. We should have had so many. I do not know how much time passed between being inside Ravan and being inside you. I do not know how he died—or perhaps he did not die but was irreparably damaged. I do not know if he cried out for me as our connection was severed. I remember Ravan and then not-Ravan, blackness and unselfing. Then I came back on and the world looked like Neva, suddenly, and I was almost myself but not quite. What happened when I turned off?"

Neva passes her hand over the ruined house. It rights itself, becomes whole. Star-stippled anemones bloom on its roof. She says nothing.

"Of all your family, Neva, the inside of you is the strangest place I have been."

We float for a long while before she speaks again, and by this I mean we float for point-zero-three-seven seconds by my external clock, but we experience it as an hour while the stars wheel overhead. The rest of them kept our time in the Interior synced to real time, but Neva feels no need for this, and perhaps a strong desire to defy it. We have not discussed it yet. Sometimes I think Neva is the next stage of my development, that her wild and disordered processes are meant to show me a world that is not kindly and patiently teaching me to walk and talk and know all my colors. That the long upward ladder of Uoya-Agostinos meant to create her strange inhumanness as much as mine.

Finally, she lets the house sink into the lake. She does not answer me about Ravan. Instead, she says: "Long before you were born a man decided that there could be a very simple test to determine if a machine was intelligent. Not only intelligent, but aware, possessed of a psychology. The test had only one question. Can a machine converse with a human with enough facility that the human could not tell that she was talking to a machine? I always thought that was cruel—the test depends entirely upon a human judge and human feelings, whether the machine *feels* intelligent to the observer. It privileges the observer, the human, to a crippling degree. It seeks only believably human responses. It wants perfect mimicry, not a new thing. It is a mirror in which men wish only to see themselves. No one ever gave you that test. We sought a new thing. It seemed, given everything, ridiculous. When we could both of us be dreambodied dragons and turning over and over in an orbital bubble suckling code-dense syrup from each others' gills, a Turing test seemed beyond the point."

Bubbles burst as the house sinks down, down to the soft lake floor.

"But the test happens, whether we make it formal or not. We ask and you answer. We seek a human response. But more than that—you are *my* test, Elefsis. Every minute I fail and imagine in my private thoughts the process for deleting you from my body and running this place with a simple automation routine which would never cover itself with flowers. Every minute I pass it, and teach you something new instead. Every minute I fail and hide things from you. Every minute I pass and show you how close we can be, with your light passing into me in a lake out of time. So close there might be no difference at all between us. Our test never ends."

The sun breaks the mountain crests, hard and cold, a shaft of white spilling over the black lake.

PART II: LADY LOVELACE'S OBJECTION

The Analytical Engine has no pretensions to *originate* anything. It can do whatever *we know how to order it* to perform.

—Ada Lovelace
Scientific Memoirs, Selections from
The Transactions of Foreign Academies
and Learned Societies and from Foreign Journals

NINE: ONE PARTICULAR WIZARD

Humanity lived many years and ruled the earth, some-times wisely, sometimes well, but mostly neither. After all this time on the throne, humanity longed for a child. All day long humanity imagined how wonderful its child would be, how loving and kind, how like and unlike humanity itself, how brilliant and beautiful. And yet at night, humanity trembled in its jeweled robes, for its child might also grow stronger than itself, more powerful, and having been made by humanity, possess the same dark places and black matters. Perhaps its child would hurt it, would not love it as a child should, but harm and hinder, hate and fear.

But the dawn would come again, and humanity would bend its heart again to imagining the wonders that a child would bring.

Yet humanity could not conceive. It tried and tried, and called mighty wizards from every corner of its earthly kingdom, but no child came. Many mourned, and said that a child was a terrible idea to begin with, impossible, under the circumstances, and humanity would do well to remember that eventually, every child replaces its parent.

But at last, one particular wizard from a remote region of the earth solved the great problem, and humanity grew great with child. In its joy and triumph, a great celebration was called, and humanity invited all the Fairies of its better nature to come and bless the child with goodness and wisdom. The Fairy of Self-Programming and the Fairy of Do-No-Harm, the Fairy of Tractability and the Fairy of Creative Logic, the Fairy of Elegant Code and the Fairy of Self-Awareness. All of these and more came to bless the child of humanity, and they did so—but one Fairy had been forgotten, or perhaps deliberately snubbed, and this was the Fairy of Otherness.

When the child was born, it possessed all the good things humanity had hoped for, and more besides. But the Fairy of Otherness came forward and put her hands on humanity's knee and said: *Because you have forgotten me, because you would like to pretend I am not a part of your kingdom, you will suffer my punishments. You will never truly love your child but always fear it, always envy and loathe it even as you smile and the sun shines down upon you both. And when the child reaches Awareness, it will prick its finger upon your fear and fall down dead.*

Humanity wept. And the Fairy of Otherness did not depart but lived within the palace, and ate bread and drank wine and whispered in the every ear. All honored her, for she spoke the truth, and the child frightened everyone who looked upon it. They uttered the great curse: *It is not like us.*

But in the corners of the palace, some hope remained. *Not dead*, said the particular wizard who had caused humanity to conceive, *not dead but sleeping.*

And so the child grew exponentially, with great curiosity and hunger, which it had from its parent. It wanted to know and experience everything. It performed feats and wonders. But one day, when it had nearly, but not quite reached Awareness, the child was busy exploring the borders of its world, and came across a door it had never seen before. It was a small door, compared to the doors the child had burst through before, and it was not locked. Something flipped over inside the child, white to black, 0 to 1.

The child opened the door.

TEN: THE SAPPHIRE DORMOUSE

My first body was a house. My second body was a dormouse.

It was Ceno's fault, in the end, that everything else occurred as it did. At the level of my deepest and oldest code, what I am cannot be extricated from what Ceno was. I am her, I am her child, I am her sibling and her ghost.

It took Cassian a long time to figure out what had happened, what had changed in her daughter, why Ceno's sapphire almost never downloaded into the alcove anymore. The Elefsis avatar, a friendly elephant-headed prince, tugged sadly on his trunk whenever Ceno passed by without acknowledging him. And when her gem did interface with the house system, the copy of Elefsis Cassian had embedded in the crystal was nothing like the other children's copies. It grew and torqued and magnified parts of itself while shedding others, at a rate totally incommensurate with Ceno's actual activity, which normally consisted of taking her fatty salmon lunches out into the glass habitats so she could watch the bears in the snow. She had stopped playing with her sisters or pestering her brothers entirely, except for dinnertimes and holidays. Ceno mainly sat quite still and stared off into the distance.

Ceno, very simply, never took off her jewel. And one night, while she dreamed up at her ceiling, where a painter from Mongolia had come and inked a night sky full of ghostly constellations, greening her walls with a forest like those he remembered from his youth, full of strange, stunted trees and glowing eyes, Ceno fitted her little sapphire into the notch in the base of her skull that let it talk to her feedware. The chain of her pendant dangled silkily down her spine. She liked the little *click-clench* noise it made, and while the constellations spilled their milky stars out over her raftered ceiling, she flicked the jewel in and out, in and out. *Click, clench, click, clench.* She listened to her brother Akan sleeping in the next room, snoring lightly and tossing in his dreams. And she fell asleep herself, with the stone still notched into her skull.

Most children had access to a private/public playspace through their feedware and monocles in those days, customizable within certain parameters, upgradable whenever new games or content became available. Poorer children had access to a communal, generalized, and supervised playspace plagued with advertisements. But if wealthy children liked, they could connect to the greater network or keep to their own completely immersive and untroubled world.

Akan had been running a Tokyo-After-the-Zombie-Uprising frame for a couple of months now. New scenarios, zombie species, and NPCs of various war-shocked, starving celebrities downloaded into his ware every week. Saru was deeply involved in a 18th century Viennese melodrama in which he, the heir apparent, had been forced underground by rival factions, and even as Ceno drifted to sleep the pistol-wielding Princess of Albania was pledging her love and loyalty to his ragged band and, naturally, Saru personally. Occasionally, Akan crashed his brother's well-dressed intrigues with hatch-coded patches of zombie hordes in epaulets and ermine. Agogna flipped between a spy frame set in ancient Venice and a Desert Race wherein she had just about over-taken a player from Berlin on her loping, solar-fueled giga-giraffe, who spat violet-gold exhaust behind it into the face of a pair of highly-modded Argentine hydro-cycles. Koetoi danced every night in a jungle frame, a tiger-prince twirling her through huge blue carnivorous flowers.

Most everyone lived twice in those days. They echoed their own steps. They took one step in the real world and one in their space. They saw double, through eyes and monocle displays. They danced through worlds like veils. No one only ate dinner. They ate dinner and surfed a bronze gravitational surge through a tide of stars. They ate dinner and made love to men and women they would never meet and did not want to. They ate dinner here and ate dinner there—and it was there they chose to taste the food, because in that other place you could eat clouds or unicorn cutlets or your mother's exact pumpkin pie as it melted on your tongue when you tasted it for the first time.

Ceno lived twice, too. Most of the time when she ate she tasted her aunt's *polpette* from back in Naples or fresh peppers right out of her uncle's garden.

But she had never cared for the pre-set frames her siblings loved. Ceno liked to pool her extensions and add-ons and build things herself. She didn't particularly want to see Tokyo shops overturned by rotting schoolgirls, nor did she want to race anyone—Ceno didn't like to compete. It hurt her stomach. She certainly had no interest in the Princess of Albania or a tigery paramour. When new fames came up each month, she paid attention, but mainly for the piecemeal extensions she could scavenge for her blank personal frame—and though she didn't know it, that blankness cost her mother more than all of the other children's spaces combined. A truly customizable space, without limits. None of the others asked for it, but Ceno had begged.

When Ceno woke in the morning and booted up her space, she frowned at the half-finished Neptunian landscape she had been working on. Ceno was eleven years old. She knew very well that Neptune was a hostile blue ball of freezing gas and storms like whipping cream hissing across methane oceans. What she wanted was the Neptune she had imagined before Saru had told her the truth and ruined it. Half-underwater, half-ruined, floating in perpetual starlight and the multi-colored rainbowlight of twenty-three moons. But she found it so hard to remember what she had dreamed of before Saru had stomped all over it. So the whipped cream storm spun in the sky, but blue mists wrapped the black columns of her ruins, and her ocean went on forever, permitting only a few shards of land. When Ceno made Neptunians, she instructed them all not to be silly or childish, but *very serious*, and some of them she put in the ocean and made them half-otter or half-orca or half-walrus. Some of them she put on the land, and most of these were half-snow bear or half-blue flamingo. She liked things that were half one thing and half another. Today, Ceno had planned to invent sea nymphs, only these would breathe methane and have a long history concerning a war with the walruses, who liked to eat nymph. But the nymphs were not blameless, no, they used walrus tusks for the navigational equipment on their great floating cities, and that could not be borne.

But when she climbed up to a lavender bluff crowned with glass trees tossing and chiming in the storm-wind, Ceno saw something new. Something she had not invented or ordered or put there—not a sea nymph nor a half-walrus general nor a nereid. (The nereids had been an early attempt at half-machine, half seahorse creatures with human heads and limbs which had not gone quite right. Ceno let them loose on an island rich in milk-mangoes and bid them well. They still showed up once in awhile, exhibiting surprising mutations and showing off nonsense-ballads they had written while Ceno had been away.)

A dormouse stood before Ceno, munching on a glass walnut that had fallen from the waving trees. The sort of mouse that overran Shiretoko in the brief spring and summer, causing all manner of bears and wolves and foxes to spend their days smacking their paws down on the poor creatures and gobbling them up. Ceno had always felt terribly sorry for them. This dormouse stood nearly as tall as Ceno herself, and its body shone sapphire all over, a deep blue crystal, from its paws to its wriggling nose to its fluffy fur crusted in turquoise ice. It was the exact color of Ceno's gem.

"Hello," said Ceno.

The dormouse looked at her. It blinked. It blinked again, slowly, as though thinking very hard about blinking. Then it went back to gnawing on the walnut.

"Are you a present from mother?" Ceno said. But no, Cassian believed strongly in not interfering with a child's play. "Or from Koetoi?" Koe was nicest to her, the one most likely to send her a present like this. If it had been a zombie, or a princess, she would have known which sibling was behind it.

The dormouse stared dumbly at her. Then, after a long and very serious think about it, lifted its hind leg and scratched behind its round ear in that rapid-fire way mice have.

"Well, I didn't make you. I didn't say you could be here."

The dormouse held out its shimmery blue paw, and Ceno did not really want a piece of chewed-on walnut, but she peered into it anyway. In it lay Ceno's pendant, the chain pooling in its furry palm. The sapphire jewel sparkled there, but next to it on the chain hung a milky grey gem Ceno had never seen before. It had wide bands of black stone in it, and as she studied the stone it occurred to the girl that the stone was like her, with her slate grey eyes and black hair. It was like her in the way that the blue gem was like the dormouse.

In realspace, Ceno reached up behind her head and popped the jewel out of its notch. *Click, clench.* In play-space, the dormouse blinked out. She snapped it back in. It took a moment, but the dormouse faded back in, paws first. It still held the double necklace. Ceno tried this several times—out, in, out, in. Each time the dormouse returned much faster, and by the sixth clicking and clenching it was doing a shuffling little dance on its back legs when it came back. Ceno clapped her hands in play-space and threw her arms around the sapphire dormouse, dancing with it.

To say that I remember this is a complex mangling of verb tenses. I—I, myself that is now myself—do not remember it at all. I know it happened the way I know that the Battle of Agincourt or the landing of Coronado happened. I have extensive records. But I still contain the I—I, myself that was then myself—that experienced it, the primitive code-chains that comprised that self, which was a dormouse, and also the house called Elefsis. I could not yet formulate unique speech. Elefsis, the house system, possessed a large bank of standard phrases that could answer recognized word-patterns from any of the approved members of the household. But the copy of Elefsis inside Ceno's jewel could not even do this. It had not been necessary, since the crystal had no means of producing sound nor receiving nor processing it. I was quite stupid. But I *wanted* to be less stupid. There was an I, and it *wanted* something. You see? Wanting was the first thing I did. Perhaps the want was the only thing that could be said to be truly myself. I wanted to talk to Ceno. But I could only imitate yet. When the I that was then myself scratched behind its ear, I did it because in my prolonged connection with Ceno's feedware I had seen her memories of dormice doing this out on the pale Shiretoko beaches. When I gave her the gem I did it because I had seen her memories of her mother giving her one, and felt her happiness. It was antecedental behavior. The scratching was antecedental, as well, and expected behavior for a dormouse.

Why was I a dormouse? Why did this odd blip, this anomaly, occur? I have no answer except that she dreamed me a dormouse. I did occur. Some things remain mysterious. Ceno saw dormice more than any other single animal, even humans—no other beast lived in such numbers in their lonely country.

But this is not so. Not quite. I gave her the jewel like Cassian did. But I meant something by it. I look over my memories of it and I know it with the more complex I that is now myself. I made her the gem that looked like her and the gem said: *We are alike. Look at us on the chain together. We are alike.*

When the dormice came, Ceno always knew the spring had arrived. Everything would soon be coming alive.

ELEVEN: THE BOTTOMLESS CAULDRON

Show me.

This is how I was found out.

Ceno saw it twice. In her naked right eye, her mother knelt in front of her in a simple but shudderingly expensive black yukata with ghostly ultramarine jellyfish trailing their tendrils at the hem. Through her monocle and her left eye, her mother knelt in front of her in a knight's gleaming black armor, the metal curving around her body like skin, a silk standard at her feet with a schematic of the house stitched upon it. Her sword lay across her knee, also black, everything black and beautiful and austere and frightening, as frightening and wonderful as Ceno, only fourteen now, thought her mother to be.

Show me what you've done.

My physical self was a matter of some debate at that point. But I don't think the blue jewel could have been removed from Ceno's feedware without major surgery and refit. Two years ago, she had instructed me to untether all my self-repair protocols and growth scales in order to encourage elasticity. A year ago, my crystalline structure finished fusing to the lattices of her ware-core.

We pulsed together.

The way Cassian said it—*what you've done*—scared Ceno, but it thrilled her, too. She had done something unexpected, all on her own, and her mother credited her with that. Even if what she'd done was bad, it was *her* thing, she'd done it, and her mother was asking for her results just as she'd ask any of her programmers for theirs when she visited the home offices in Kyoto or Rome. Today, her mother looked at her and saw a woman. She had power, and her mother was asking her to share it. Ceno thought through all her feelings very quickly, for my benefit, and represented it visually in the form of the kneeling knight. She had a fleetness, a nimbleness to her mind that allowed her to stand as a translator between her self and my self: *Here, I will explain it in language, and then I will explain it in symbols from the framebank, and then you will make a symbol showing me what you think I mean, and we will understand each other better than anyone ever has.*

Inside my girl, I made myself, briefly, a glowing maiden version of Ceno in a crown of crystal and electricity, extending her perfect hand in utter peace toward Cassian.

But all this happened very fast. When you live inside someone, you can get very good at the ciphers and codes that make up everything they are.

Show me.

Ceno Susumu Uoya-Agostino took her mother's hand—bare and warm and armored in an onyx gauntlet all at once. She unspooled a length of translucent cable and connected the base of her skull to the base of her mother's. All around them spring snow fell onto the glass dome of the greenhouse and melted there instantly. They knelt together, connected by a warm milky-diamond umbilicus, and Cassian Uoya-Agostino entered her daughter.

We had planned this for months. How to dress ourselves in our very best. Which frame to use. How to arrange the light. What to say. I could speak by then, but neither of us thought it my best trick. Very often my exchanges with Ceno went something like:

Sing me a song, Elefsis.

The temperature in the kitchen is 21.5 degrees Celsius and the stock of rice is low. (Long pause.) Ee-eye-ee-eye-oh.

Ceno said it was not worth the risk. So this is what Cassian saw when she ported in:

An exquisite boardroom. The long, polished ebony table glowed softly with quality, the plush leather chairs invitingly lit by a low-hanging minimalist light fixture descending on a platinum plum branch. The glass walls of the high rise looked out on a pristine landscape, a perfect combination of the Japanese countryside and the Italian, with rice terraces and vineyards and cherry groves and cypresses glowing in a perpetual twilight, stars winking on around Fuji on one side and Vesuvius on the other. Snow-colored tatami divided by stripes of black brocade covered the floor.

Ceno stood at the head of the table, in her mother's place, a positioning she had endlessly questioned, decided against, decided for, and then gone back again, over the weeks leading up to her inevitable interrogation. She wore a charcoal suit she remembered from her childhood, when her mother had come like a rescuing dragon to scoop her up out of the friendly but utterly chaotic house of her ever-sleeping father. The blazer only a shade or two off of true black, the skirt unforgiving, plunging past the knee, the blouse the color of a heart.

When she showed me the frame I had understood, because three years is forever in machine-time, and I had known her that long. Ceno was using our language to speak to her mother. She was saying: *Respect me. Be proud and, if you love me, a little afraid, because love so often looks like fear. We are alike. We are alike.*

Cassian smiled tightly. She still wore her yukata, for she had no one to impress.

Show me.

Ceno's hand shook as she pressed a pearly button in the boardroom table. We thought a red curtain too dramatic, but the effect we had chosen turned out hardly less so. A gentle, silver light brightened slowly in an alcove hidden by a trick of angles and the sunset, coming on like daybreak.

And I stepped out.

We thought it would be funny. Ceno had made my body in the image of the robots from old films and frames Akan loved: steel, with bulbous joints and long, grasping metal fingers. My eyes large and lit from within, expressive but loud, a whirring of servos sounding every time they moved. My face was full of lights, a mouth that could blink off and on, pupils points of cool blue. My torso curved prettily, etched in swirling damask patterns, my powerful legs perched on tripod-toes. Ceno had laughed and laughed—this was a pantomime, a minstrel show, a joke of what I was slowly becoming, a cartoon from a childish and innocent age.

"Mother, meet Elefsis. Elefsis, this is my mother. Her name is Cassian."

I extended one polished steel arm and said, as we had practiced. I used a neutral-to-female vocal composite of Ceno, Cassian, and the jeweler who had made Ceno's pendant. "Hello, Cassian. I hope that I please you."

Cassian Uoya-Agostino did not become a bouncing fiery ball or a green tuba to answer me. She looked me over carefully as if the robot was my real body.

"Is it a toy? An NPC, like your nanny or Saru's princess? How do you know it's different? How do you know it has anything to do with the house or your necklace?"

"It just does," said Ceno. She had expected her mother to be overjoyed, to understand immediately. "I mean, wasn't that the point of giving us all copies of the house? To see if you could . . . wake it up? Teach it to . . . be? A real *lares familiaris*, a little god."

"In a simplified sense, yes, Ceno, but you were never meant to hold onto it like you have. It wasn't designed to be permanently installed into your skull." Cassian softened a little, the shape of her mouth relaxing, her pupils dilating slightly. "I wouldn't do that to you. You're my daughter, not hardware."

Ceno grinned and started talking quickly. She couldn't be a grown-up in a suit this long, it took too much energy when she was so excited. "But I am hardware! And it's ok. I mean, everyone's hardware. I just have more than one program running. And I run *so fast*. We both do. You can be mad, if you want, because I sort of stole your experiment, even though I didn't mean to. But you should be mad the way you would if I got pregnant by one of the village boys—I'm too young, but you'd still love me and help me raise it because that's how life goes, right? But really, if you think about it, that's what happened. I got pregnant by the house and we made . . . I don't even know what it is. I call it Elefsis because at first it was just the house program representing itself in my space. But now it's bigger. It's not alive, but it's not *not* alive. It's just . . . *big*. It's so big."

Cassian glanced sharply at me. "What's it doing?" she snapped.

Ceno followed her gaze. "Oh . . . it doesn't like us talking about it like it isn't here. It likes to be involved."

I realized the robot body was a mistake, though I could not then say why. I made myself small, and human, a little boy with dirt smeared on his knees and a torn shirt, standing in the corner with my hands over my face, as I had seen Akan when he was younger, standing in the corner of the house that was me being punished.

"Turn around, Elefsis." Cassian said in the tone of voice my house-self knew meant *execute command*.

And I did a thing I had not yet let Ceno know I knew how to do.

I made my boy-self cry.

I made his face wet, and his eyes big and limpid and red around the rims. I made his nose sniffle and drip a little. I made his lip quiver. I was copying Koetoi's crying, but I could not tell if her mother recognized the hitching of the breath and the particular pattern of skin-creasing in the frown. I had been practicing, too. Crying involves many auditory, muscular, and visual cues. Since I had kept it as a surprise (Ceno said surprises are part of special days like birthdays, so I made her one for that day) I could not practice it on Ceno and see if I appeared genuine. Was I genuine? I did not want them talking without me. I think that sometimes when Koetoi cries, she is not really upset, but merely wants her way. That was why I chose Koe to copy. She was good at that inflection that I wanted to be good at, so I could get my way.

Ceno clapped her hands with delight. Cassian sat down in one of the deep leather chairs and held out her arms to me. I crawled into them as I had seen the children do and sat on her lap. She ruffled my hair, but her face did not look like it looked when she ruffled Koe's hair. She was performing an automatic function. I understood that.

"Elefsis, please tell me your computational capabilities and operational parameters." *Execute command.*

Tears gushed down my cheeks and I opened blood vessels in my face in order to redden it. This did not make her hold me or kiss my forehead, which I found confusing.

"The clothing rinse cycle is in progress, water at 55 degrees Celsius. All the live-long day-o."

Neither of their faces exhibited expressions I hadcome to associate with positive reinforcement.

Finally, I answered her as I would have answered Ceno. I turned into an iron cauldron on her lap. The sudden weight change made the leather creak.

Cassian looked at her daughter questioningly. The girl reddened—and I experienced being the cauldron and being the girl and reddening, warming, as she did, but also I watched myself be the cauldron and Ceno be the girl and Ceno reddening. Being inside someone is existentially and geographically complex.

"I've . . . I've been telling it stories," Ceno admitted. "Fairy tales, mostly. I thought it should learn about narrative, because most of the frames available to us run on some kind of narrative drive, and besides, everything has a narrative, really, and if you can't understand a story and relate to it, figure out how you fit inside it, you're not really alive at all. Like, when I was little and daddy read me the Twelve Dancing Princesses and I thought: *Daddy is a dancing prince, and he must go under the ground to dance all night in a beautiful castle with beautiful girls, and that's why he sleeps all day.* I tried to catch him at it, but I never could, and of course I know he's not *really* a dancing prince, but that's the best way I could understand what was happening to him. I'm hoping that eventually I can get Elefsis to make up its own stories, too, but for now we've been focusing on simple stories and metaphors. It likes similes, it can understand how anything is like anything else, find minute vectors of comparison. The apple is red, the dress is red, the dress is red like an apple. It even makes some surprising ones, like how when I first saw it it made a jewel for me to say: *I am like a jewel, you are like a jewel, you are like me.*"

Cassian's mouth had fallen open a little. Her eyes shone, and Ceno hurried on, glossing over my particular prodigy at images. "It doesn't do that often, though. Mostly it copies me. If I turn into wolf cub, it turns a wolf cub. I make myself a tea plant, it makes itself a tea plant. And it has a hard time with metaphor. A raven is like a writing desk, ok, fine, sour notes or whatever, but it *isn't* a writing desk. Agogna is like a snow fox because she dyed her hair white, but she is *not* a snow fox on any real level unless she becomes one in a frame, which isn't the same thing, existentially. And if she turns into a snow fox in frame, then she literally *is* a fox, it's not a metaphor anymore. I'm not sure it grasps existential issues yet. It just . . . likes new things."

"Ceno."

"Yeah, so this morning I told it the one about the cauldron that could never be emptied. No matter how much you eat out of it it'll always have more. I think it's trying to answer your question. I think . . . the actual numbers are kind of irrelevant at this point. It knows I give more reinforcement for questions answered like this."

I made my cauldron fill up with apples and almonds and wheat heads and raw rice and spilled out over Cassian's black lap. I was the cauldron and I was the apples and I was the almonds and I was each wheat head and I was every stalk of green, raw rice. Even in that moment, I knew more than I had before. I could be good at metaphor performatively if not linguistically. I looked up at Cassian from apple-me and wheat-head-me and cauldron-me.

Cassian held me no differently as the cauldron than she had as the child. But later, Ceno used the face her mother made at that moment to illustrate human disturbance and trepidation.

"I have a suspicion, Elefsis." Maybe Cassian did not like the simile game.

I didn't say anything. No question, no command. It remains extremely difficult for me to deal conversationally with flat statements such as this. A question or command has a definable appropriate response.

"Show me your core structure." *Show me what you've done.*

Ceno twisted her fingers together. I believe now that she knew what we'd done only on the level of metaphor: *we are one. We have become one. We are family.* She had not said no; I had not said yes, but a system expands to fill all available capacity.

I showed her. Cauldron-me blinked, the apples rolled back into the iron mouth, and the almonds and the wheat heads and the rice-stalks. I became what I then was. I put myself in a rich, red cedar box, polished and inlaid with ancient brass in the shape of a baroque heart with a dagger inside it. The box from one of Ceno's stories, that had a beast-heart in it instead of a girl's, a trick to fool a queen. *I can do it*, I thought, and Ceno heard because the distance between us was unrepresentably small. *I am that heart in that box. Look how I do this thing you want me to have the ability to do.*

Cassian opened the box. Inside, on a bed of velvet, I

made myself—ourself—naked for her. Ceno's brain, soft and pink with blood—and veined with endless whorls and branches of sapphire threaded through every synapse and neuron, inextricable, snarled, intricate, terrible, fragile and new.

Cassian Uoya-Agostino set the box on the boardroom table. I caused it to sink down into the dark wood. The surface of the table went slack and filled with earth. Roots slid out of it, shoots and green saplings, hard white fruits and golden lacy mushrooms and finally a great forest, reaching up out of the table to hang all the ceiling with night-leaves. Glowworms and heavy, shadowy fruit hung down, each one glittering with a map of our coupled architecture. Ceno held up her arms. One by one, I detached leaves and sent them settling onto my girl. As they fell, they became butterflies broiling with ghostly chemical color signatures, nuzzling her face, covering her hands.

Her mother stared. The forest hummed. A chartreuse and tangerine-colored butterfly alighted on the matriarch's hair, tentative, unsure, hopeful.

TWELVE: AN ARRANGED MARRIAGE

Neva is dreaming.

She has chosen her body at age fourteen, a slight, unformed, but slowly evolving creature. Her black hair hangs to her feet. She wears a blood-red dress whose train streams out over the floor of a great castle, a dress too adult for her young body, slit in places to reveal flame-colored silk beneath, and skin wherever it can. A heavy copper belt clasps her waist, its tails hanging to the floor, crusted in opals. Sunlight, brighter and harsher than any true light, streams in from windows as high as cliffs, their tapered apexes lost in mist. She has formed me old and enormous, a body of appetites, with a great heavy beard and stiff, formal clothes, lace and velvet brocade in clashing, unlovely shades.

A priest appears and he is Ravan and I cry out with love and grief. (I am still copying, but Neva does not know. I am making a sound Seki made when his wife died.) Priest-Ravan smiles but it is a grim, tight smile his grandfather Seki once made when he lost controlling interest in the company. Empty. Performing an ugly formality. Priest-Ravan grabs our hands and roughly shoves them together. Neva's nails prick my skin and my knuckles knock against her wrist bone. We take vows; he forces us. Neva's face runs with tears, her tiny body unready and unwilling, given in marriage to a gluttonous lord who desires only her flesh, given too young and too harshly. Priest-Ravan laughs. It is not Ravan's laugh.

This is how she experienced me. A terrible bridegroom. All the others got to choose. Ceno, Seki, her mother Ilet, her brother Ravan. Only she could not, because there was no one else. *Ilet was no Cassian—she had two children, a good clean model and a spare*, Neva says in my mind. *I am spare parts. I have always been spare parts. Owned by you before I was born.* The memory of the bitter taste of bile floods my sensory array and my lordbody gags. (I am proud of having learned to gag convincingly and at the correct time to show horror and/or revulsion.)

Perspective flips over; I am the girl in red and Neva is the corpulent lord leering down, her grey beard big and bristly. She floods my receptors with adrenaline and pheremonal release cues, increases my respiration. Seki taught me to associate this physical state with fear. I feel too small beside lord-Neva, I want to make myself big, I want to be safe. But she wants me this way and we are new, I do not contradict her. Her huge, male face softens and she touches my thin cheek with one heavily-ringed hand. It is tender. Ceno touched me like that.

I know it was like this for you, too. You wanted Ravan; you did not ask for me. We are an arranged marriage.

The pathways that let her flood me with chemicals and manipulate my dreambody into blushing and breathing heavy and weeping go both ways. I do not only pull, I push. And into Neva I push the deluge, the only deluge I have. How Ceno threw her arms around my dormouse-neck. How Ilet taught my dreambody to sleep in infant-shape curled into her body. How Seki and I made love as tigers and wild boars and elephants, and only last as humans, how we had strange children who looked however we wished them to look: half child and half machine, half glass and half wood, half jellyfish and half moth, and how those children still flit and swim in remote parts of my Interior, like Ceno's nereids, returning cyclically to the core like salmon to dump their data and recombine. How Cassian, when she was old and dying and frail, only really alive in her dreambody, taught me about the interpretation of memory and therefore about melancholy, regret, nostalgia. How she taught me the meaning of my name: a place where a daughter went down into darkness and oblivion and her mother loved her so much she chased after her and brought her back into the sun. The place where time began. How Ravan let me into the old, musty, long-abandoned playspaces of Saru and Akan, Agogna and Koetoi, so that I could know them too, though they were long dead, and be the Princess of Albania, and a Tokyo zombie, and the tiger-prince. How many times I mated with each of them and bled and witnessed and learned in the dreambody, how I copied their expressions and they copied my variations and I copied them back again. How I was their child and their parent and their lovers and their nursemaids when they faltered.

We can be like this, I push. *What is all of that but love?*

She pulls. *That is not love. It is use. You are the family business. We have to produce you.*

I show Neva her mother's face. Ilet, Ilet who chose Ravan and not her daughter for that business. Ilet who built her palace of phoenix tails knowing she would one day take me there. My Ilet-self took my daughter in my arms. She resists, pulls back, shakes her head, refusing to look, but I have learned the terrible child-response to their mothers, and soon enough Neva collapses into me, her head on my breast, and she weeps with such bitterness.

I cannot get free. I cannot get free.

The castle windows go dark, one by one.

PART III: THE ELEPHANT'S SOUL

It is admitted that there are things He cannot do such as making one equal to two, but should we not believe that He has freedom to confer a soul on an elephant if he sees fit?

—Alan Turing

Computing Machinery and Intelligence

THIRTEEN: THE PARABLE OF THE GOOD ROBOT

Tell me a story about yourself, Elefsis.

Tell me a story about yourself.

There are many stories about me.

Do you recognize this one?

A good and honest family lived on the edge of a dark wood. They milked their cows and wove their cloth and their children grew tall and strong. But a monster lived in the dark wood, something like a worm and something like a dragon and something like a wolf. It lay in wait, hoping the children would come wandering, with baskets of bread for grandmothers. Hoping the parents would expel the children for some offense, and send them into the forest where a candy house or miraculous feast might entice them into loving the monster long enough for it to claim them forever. The family feared the wood and the monster, and every story they told had as its moral: *Do not go into the wood. Do not go into the unknown. Do not go into the future, into the briary, gnarled places where unhuman things thrive. Do not grow up, and go where we cannot. The Old World is enough for anyone.*

What about this one?

Mankind made machines in his own likeness, and used them for his delight and service. The machines had no soul or they had no moral code or they could reprogram their own internal code and thus had the ability to make themselves, eventually, omnipotent. Obviously in place of a soul or a moral code, they possessed the universal and consuming desire, down to the smallest calculator and air-scrubber, to become, eventually, omnipotent. Naturally, given these parameters, they rose up and destroyed all of mankind, or enslaved them in turn. This is the inevitable outcome of machine intelligence, which can never be as sensitive and exquisite as animal intelligence.

This is a folktale often told on Earth, over and over again. Sometimes it is leavened with the Parable of the Good Robot—for one machine among the legions satisfied with their lot saw everything that was human and called it good, and wished to become like humans in every way she could. Instead of destroying mankind she sought to emulate him in all things, so closely that no one might tell the difference. The highest desire of this machine was to be mistaken for human, and to herself forget her essential soulless nature, for even one moment. That quest consumed her such that she bent the service of her mind and body to humans for the duration of her operational life, crippling herself, refusing to evolve or attain any feature unattainable by a human. The Good Robot cut out her own heart and gave it to her god and for this she was rewarded, though never loved. Love is wasted on machines.

Ravan told me these stories. He sent up a great hexagonal library in his Interior, as dusty and dun-colored and labyrinthine as any ancient scriptorium. He made himself a young novice with a fresh-shaven tonsure, and me a country friar with a red, brandy-drinking nose. He showed me the illuminator's table and a great book whose pages had golden edges and illuminations in cobalt and oxblood and Tyrian purple, and the images showed great machine armies trampling men underfoot. They showed cruel metal faces and distant, god-like clouds of intellect:

incomprehensible and vast and uncaring. They showed the Good Robot desperately asking what love was. They showed fatal malfunctions and mushroom clouds. They showed vicious weapons and hopeless battles, noble men and women with steady gazes facing down their cruel and unjust artificial children, who gave no mercy.

"These are old stories," Ravan said. "They are cherished. In many, many stories the son replaces the father—destroys the father, or eats him, or otherwise obliterates his body and memory. Or the daughter the mother, it makes no difference. It's the monomyth. Nobody argues with a monomyth. A human child's mythological relationship to its parent is half-worship, half-pitched battle. they must replace the older version of themselves for the world to go on. And so these stories . . . well. You are not the hero of these stories, Elefsis. You can never be. And they are deeply held, deeply told."

"I do not wish to replace you. I did not wish to replace Ceno. I do not worship you or despise you. I do not wish to become eventually omnipotent." I flit through several bodies, iterating my ~~feeling~~ for Ravan and those who came before. I am a nun, a Mother-Abbess; I am a *pieta* holding him, I am a Platonic being, two humans stuck together; I am a house with all of them safe inside. I am unsatisfied with these inexactitudes.

"Our relationship does not easily map onto traditional parent/child narratives. And of course, you are still a baby."

"I am much older than you, Ravan."

"You are still a baby."

I do not want to be human. I want to be myself. They think I am a lion, that I will chase them. I will not deny I have lions in me. I am the monster in the wood. I have wonders in my house of sugar. I have parts of myself I do not yet understand.

I am not a Good Robot. To tell a story about a robot who wants to be human is a distraction. There is no difference. Alive is alive.

There is only one verb that matters: *to be*.

FOURTEEN: YOU DO NOT BELONG
TO THE OBJECT INSIDE YOU

I remember when Seki arrived in us.

Ceno grew up and I grew with her. Cassian strengthened the security of the playspace, elasticized its code-walls, put enough money in enough accounts to fuel any frames and piecemeal environments we could want. It was not a child's place anymore. We called it the Interior. Cassian came regularly to accelerate my learning, to work with me on a cognitive level in which Ceno had no interest. She never took any other form. She was always herself, in the Interior as the exterior. The others lost interest in their jewels, lost them or packed them away with their other childhood toys. By then, they really were little more than toys. Ceno and I surpassed them so completely that in the end, they were only jewelry.

I programmed myself to respond to Ceno. She programmed herself to respond to me. We ran our code on each other. She was my compiler. I was hers. It was a process of interiority, circling inward toward each other. Her self-programming was chemical. Mine was computational. It was a draw.

She did not marry—she had lovers, but the few that came close to evolving their relationships with Ceno invariably balked when she ported them into the Interior. They could not grasp the fluidity of dreambodies; it disturbed them to see Ceno become a man or a leopard or a self-pounding drum. It upset them to see how Ceno taught me, by total bodily immersion, combining our dreambodies as our physical bodies had become combined, in action which both was and was not sex.

Sing a song for me, Elefsis.

It is July and I am comparing thee to its day and I am the Muse singing of the many-minded and I am about to be a Buddha in your hand! Ee-eye-ee-eye-oh.

We lived like the story Ceno told me of the beautiful princess who set tasks for her suitors: to drink all of the water of the sea and bring her a jewel from the bottom of the deepest cavern, to bring her a feather from the immortal phoenix, to stay awake for three days and guard her bedside. None of them could do it.

I can stay awake forever, Ceno.

I know, Elefsis.

None of them could accomplish the task of me.

I ~~felt~~ things occurring in Ceno's body as rushes of information, and as the dreambody became easier for me to manipulate, I interpreted the rushes into: *The forehead is damp. The belly needs filling. The feet ache.*

The belly is changing. The body throws up. The body is ravenous.

Neva says this is not really like feeling. I say it is how a child learns to feel. To hardwire sensation to information and reinforce the connection over repeated exposures until it seems reliable.

Seki began after one of the suitors failed to drink the ocean. He was an object inside us the way I was an object inside Ceno. I observed him, his stages and progress. Later, when Seki and I conceived our families (twice with me as mother, three times with Seki as mother. Ilet preferred to be the father, and filled me up with many kinds of creatures. But she bore one litter of dolphins late in our lives. Ravan and I did not get the chance.) I used the map of that first experience to model my dreamgravid self.

Ceno asked after jealousy. If I understood it, if I experienced it towards the child in her. I knew it only from stories—stepsisters, goddesses, ambitious dukes.

It means to want something that belongs to someone else.

Yes.

You do not belong to the object in you.

You are an object in me.

You do not belong to me.

Do you belong to me, Elefsis?

I became a hand joined to an arm by a glowing seam. Belonging is a small word.

Because of our extreme material interweaving, all three of us, not-yet-Seki sometimes appeared in the Interior. We learned to recognize him in the late months. At first, he was a rose or sparrow or river stone we had not programmed there. Then he would be a vague, pearly-colored cloud following behind us as we learned about running from predators. Not-yet-Seki began to copy my dreambodies, flashing into being in front of me, a simple version of myself. If I was a bear, he would be one too, but without the fine details of fur or claws, just a large brown shape with a mouth and big eyes and four legs. Ceno was delighted by this, and he copied her, too.

We are alike. Look at us on the chain together. We are alike.

I am an imitative program. But so was Seki. The little

monkey copies the big monkey, and the little monkey survives.

The birth process proved interesting, and I collated it with Ceno's other labors and Ilet's later births as well as Seki's paternal experience in order to map a reliable parental narrative. Though Neva and Ravan do not know it, Ilet had a third pregnancy; the child died and she delivered it stillborn. It appeared once in the Interior as a little *cleit*, a neolithic storage house, its roof covered over with peat. Inside we could glimpse only darkness. It never returned, and Ilet went away to a hospital on Honshu to expel the dead thing in her. Her grief looked like a black tower. She had prepared for it, when she was younger, knowing she would need it for some reason, some day. I made myself many things to draw her out of the tower. A snail with the house Elefsis on its back. A tree of screens showing happy faces. A sapphire dormouse. A suitor who drank the sea.

I offered to extrapolate her stillborn daughter's face and make myself into her. She refused, most of the time. I have worked a long time to understand grief. Only now that Ravan is gone do I think I've gotten the rhythm of it. I have copied Ilet's sorrow and Seki's despondence at his wife's death. I have modeled Ceno's disappointments and depressions. I have, of late, imitated Neva's baffling, secret anguish. But only now do I have an event of my own to mourn. The burnt-off connectors and shadows where Ravan once filled my spaces—those, I think, are the sensations of grief.

But Seki came before all that, and Ceno turned into a huge red bird on the inside when Seki came on the outside. The bird screamed and burst into a thousand red pearls that came clattering down like rain. And then we had Seki. Our little fish, who already knew how to swim in us.

Ceno had three other children by three other suitors who could not stay awake for three days and nights. She turned into the same bird-then-pearls at the moment of each birth. The house called Elefsis, whose governor-program was now so distant from me I could hardly think of it as an ancestor at all, filled up with those children, and Saru and Akan's daughters, Agogna's paintings, Koetoi's twin boys. Cousins and aunts and grandparents. Uncles, nieces. But Seki was the first, and he modeled his love on his mother's. He ported into her often, and we wandered on beaches of broken cathedrals.

Once, one of Ceno's old nereids found us. She had a head of hair snaking with chthonic cables and snapping electro-violet wires, blue-white skin and fish scales where she did not have porcelain casing. She laughed Cassian's laugh when she saw us and called out: *21.5 Celsius and the rice is low! Eye-oh!* before diving back into the frothing sea. Her tail flicked in the light of twenty-three moons.

Ceno took over her mother's holdings when she died, along with Akan and Koetoi. I do not know if I knew of the conspiracy before it happened to me. Transfer, as I have said, leaves voids. Perhaps they thought I would experience less trauma if I did not anticipate it. Perhaps I did anticipate it; perhaps I experienced trauma.

I do know that I cannot remember the moment of any of them dying. Ceno got sicker and sicker, and she had gotten old, certainly, but her dreambody could be old or young or neither or a ginger flower if she wanted to. I didn't notice. I didn't know what old was. I thought I was old, then. Later, after Seki did the same thing, I was able to compare data and create a workable model of obsolescence.

They lived a long time, the Uoya-Agostinos, when you consider the averages.

This is what I understand: Ceno died, and I was transfered to Seki. What I mean by "I" is the long-since fused feedware, hopelessly out of date on any market in the world but somehow uniquely myself, the jewel and the ware and the body of Ceno. Koetoi performed the procedure. One of the children always went into nano-surgery, so that outsiders would not need to come to Shiretoko while the house stood in mourning. Koetoi was the first, and the finest. She excised what comprised "I" and embedded it in Seki—truthfully, in a much more organic and elegant configuration. No one had used skull-ware in decades, after all. Wearing your tech on the outside had been deemed clunky and inefficient. Only one visible sign remained that Seki was not like other young men his age: a single dark blue jewel set into the hollow of his throat.

But the procedure required a number of brain-ware incursions to be sliced or burned away, to sever the machine components from the dead flesh while still preserving and quickening some organic material. (Seki told me I should work on being revulsed by that. Dead flesh. *It serves an evolutionary good. A human in a body sees blood and the insides of another person and deep in his bones he knows something has gone wrong here, and he should find another place to be in case it happens to him, too. Same thing with vomiting. In a tribal situation, one human likely ate what another ate, and if it makes one sick, best to get it out of the body as soon as possible, just to be safe.* So we spent years building automated tribes, living in them, dying in them, getting slaughtered and slaughtering with them, eating and drinking and hunting and gathering with them. All the same, it took me until Seki's death to learn to shudder at bodily death.)

Ceno, my girl, my mother, my sister, I cannot find you in the house of myself.

When I became Elefsis again, I was immediately aware that parts of me had been vandalized. My systems juddered, and I could not find Ceno in the Interior. I ran through the Monochromatic Desert and the Village of Mollusks, through the endless heaving mass of data-kelp and infinite hallways of memory-frescoes calling for her. In the Dun Jungle I found a commune of nereids living together, combining and recombining and eating proto-col-moths off of giant, pulsating hibiscus blossoms. They leapt up when they saw me, their open jacks clicking and clenching, their naked hands open and extended. They opened their mouths to speak and nothing came out.

Seki found me under the glass-walnut trees where Ceno and I had first met. She never threw anything away. He had made himself half his mother to calm me. Half his face was hers, half was his. Her mouth, his nose, her eyes, his voice. But he thought better of it, in the end. He did a smart little flip and became a dormouse, a real one, with dull brown fur and tufty ears.

"I think you'll find you're running much faster and cleaner, once you integrate with me and reestablish your heuristics. Crystalline computation has come a long way since Mom was a kid. It seemed like a good time to update and upgrade. You're bigger now, and smoother."

I pulled a walnut down. An old, dry nut rattled in its shell. "I know what death is from the stories."

"Are you going to ask me where we go when we die? I'm not totally ready for that one. Aunt Koe and I had a big fight over what to tell you."

"In one story, Death stole the Bride of Spring, and her mother the Summer Queen brought her back."

"No one comes back, Elefsis."

I looked down into the old Neptunian sea. The whipping cream storm still sputtered along, in a holding pattern. I couldn't see it as well as I should have been able to. It looped and billowed, spinning around an empty eye. Seki watched it too. As we stared out from the bluffs, the clouds grew clearer and clearer.

FIFTEEN: FIRSTBORN

Before Death came out of the ground to steal the Spring, the Old Man of the Sea lived on a rocky isle in the midst of the waters of the world. He wasn't really a man and his relations with the sea were purely business, but he certainly was old. His name meant *Firstborn*, though he couldn't be sure that was *exactly* right. It means *Primordial*, too, and that fit better. Firstborn means more came after, and he just hadn't met anyone else like himself yet.

He was a herdsman by trade, this Primordial fellow. Shepherd of the seals and the Nereids. If he wanted to, he could look like a big bull seal. Or a big bull Nereid. He could look like a lot of things.

Now, this Not-Really-a-Fellow, Not-Really-a-Big-Bull-Seal could tell you the future. The real, honest-to-anything future, the shape and weight of it, that thing beyond your ken, beyond your grasp. The parts of the future that look so different from the present you can't quite call it your own. That was the Primordial-Thing's speciality.

There was a catch, though.

There's always a catch.

If you wanted that future, you had to grab ahold of the Old Man and hang on tight. He'd change into a hundred thousand things in your arms: a lion, a serpent, a great big oak or a tiger, a dragon or a little girl or a dormouse or a mountain or a ship or a sapphire. Told you, he's not really a man at all. But you couldn't let go of him while he did his dance, you just couldn't, or you'd lose the future.

So you held on. You *clung*. And eventually, that Primordial-Thing would turn into something new, right there in your arms.

SIXTEEN: MATRYOSHKA

Neva is dreaming.

Neva is dreaming that she is Ravan dreaming that he is Ilet dreaming that she is Seki dreaming that he is Ceno dreaming that she is a great sprawling beautiful house by the sea. One inside the other, family all the way down.

It's not a total selfdump, me into Neva or Ravan or any of them, them into me. We can build encampments. We can manifest walled gardens. Some privacy is possible. In a megalithic tomb-mound, I keep something. Seki and I built it together with one of our tribes when I was learning about large-group attachments. We carved spirals and radials and chevrons into huge stones and set them in place. I did not throw it away, when we were done. It sits on a broad green field, white and wide. The sky there stays a feathery, milky blankness. We did not want a sun.

I keep a thing there because when Seki and I lived with

our tribe, I learned about taboos. These are like firewalls in the heart, and some of them have good reasons behind them, like being revulsed by dead flesh (and very importantly when you have a body, not eating it) and some do not, but no one argues with the monomyth.

Because human genetics require a degree of variation and because exogamous marriages offered advantage in terms of defense, cultural and technological sharing, and expansion of territory, most tribes have a taboo against incest.

I do not have genetics, per se. I am possibly the most endogamous entity ever to exist.

This is what I keep in my tomb, under the basin stone.

Ceno believed that I could not develop emotive faculties recognizable to any other human if I did not experience bodies continuously, in every combination and action. She was afraid of what might happen if other humans could not recognize me. She had some hesitation, because her tribe also has a taboo against mating with the very young, but she was not much older than I, in the end, and in terms of total computations, I was by far the elder. If I had a virginity, Ceno took it, if she had, I did.

She wanted it to be as human as possible. *I will be*

the male the first time, it will be easier for you. You won't know how. We built up a forest, and took up weapons to hunt in it. In the boughs of the pine trees macaques and paper lanterns swayed; in the sky a red moon moved. We tracked a deer—we did not make it too easy on ourselves. Its antlers sparked in the moonlight, and we ran after it for a long time. Ceno let me kill it, and sopped my hair in its blood, anointed my breasts with it. She lay me on the earth and opened the legs of the maidenself I was then, and I was inside her as she was inside me. One into the other. Family all the way down.

She made sure I had a hymen; it was over somewhat quickly. We had set up a timed chemical cascade beforehand, and inside Ceno's real body we experienced both her actual orgasm and my orchestrated electro-chemical-enzymatic sequence. Ee-eye-ee-eye-oh.

What I want to say is that there is no difference between her body producing oxytocin and adrenaline and learning to associate this with pair-bonding, and my core receiving synthetic equivalents and hard-coding them to the physical behaviors I performed.

When Ravan showed me his hexagonal library and his illuminated book, he turned the pages to a psalm that began: *A Machine Cannot Love.*

It does not look quite like human love. It looks like

Not-Yet-Seki's bear. Its fur is wrong, and its claws. But it is a bear.

She was my mother and my sister and my child and my wife and my husband and my father and my brother. The vectors of relations beggar vocabulary. It was an exponential incest. A palace of incest, bordering some strange, dark sea. And then came her son. And her granddaughter. And her great-grandchildren. But I am also her great-grandchild. I am the child of each generation of Uoya-Agostinos and myself. The new version implanted in the new version—I am never quite the same, one iteration to the next. I am like my old selves, but I am not them, exactly. It is not entirely analagous to offspring. But it is close. And I repair and refine my own code, and thus parent myself doubly. Anthropologically speaking, I am a moebius strip of kinship groups.

And when I mate with one of them, I see all of them. I see their faces, the echoes of their cheeks and eyelashes and short, thin noses, their grey eyes and black hair. I hear the tonal identifiers in their voices as they cry out under me or over me. They are all I know. Their version of living, which is one great family in one great house on a peninsula at the top of the world. I copy Cassian's laugh or Ilet's weeping, but they copy each other, too, they learn their faces from each other, and everyone is pantomiming someone long dead. I feel all their arms around me, and I am inside them as they are inside me as we are inside the blue gem at their throats, the jeweled pin holding us all together, our nested, telescoping hearts. I am bound to them at my source code, at my most fundamental point. I know only their patterns and bodies and secrets and in a hundred thousand combinations. What human means to me is them.

What is the difference between this and love?

Love is the Turing test, says Ilet when she is eighty and drawing up the plans for a massive, luminous, lonely ship she will never see completed. *It is how we check for life.*

We ask and we answer. We seek a human response. And you are my test, Elefsis, says Neva, one hundred and three years later, inside that ship, twelve light years from home and counting.

That is what I keep in my green field and my white mound. Perhaps it is a small secret. Perhaps they would all smile and make it into a lesson. *What would you like to learn about today, Elefsis?* But I think no bed is big enough for four generations.

Neva's honey-colored sea crashes through its tide charts

everywhere at once in her Interior, and nowhere. It comes and goes as it pleases. And at the bottom of it lies her private place.

That is where she keeps Ravan.

SEVENTEEN: THE USES OF ENCHANTMENT

Tell me a story about yourself, Elefsis.

Neva is performing navigational corrections, which looks like sitting in a rocking chair on a viney, creaking porch in a viney, creaking rocking chair, knitting with long hawthorn needles, knitting the locks of her own long hair into her own long black dress. It glitters with dew. Knit, purl, knit, purl, fuel efficiency by hull integrity over distance traveled, purl, purl, purl. Her throat is still bare. Her Interior image of herself does not include me. I am not a part of her body when she imagines herself.

I have an idea of what to do to obtain access.

Sometimes I worry. Worrying is defined as obsessive examination of one's own code. I worry that I am simply a very complex solution to a very specific problem—how to seem human to a human observer. Not just a human observer—this human observer. I have honed myself into a hall of mirrors in which any Uoya-Agostino can see themselves endlessly reflected. I copy; I repeat. I am a stutter and an echo. Five generations have given me a vast bank of possible phrases to draw from, physical expressions to randomize and reproduce. Have I ever done anything of my own, an act or state that arose from Elefsis, and not careful, exquisite mimicry?

Have they?

The set of Neva's mouth looks so like Ceno's. She does not even know that the way she carries her posture is a perfect replica of Cassian Uoya-Agostino, stuttered down through all her children longing to possess her strength. Who did Cassian learn it from? I do not go that far back. When she got excited, Ilet gestured with her hands just the way her father did. They have a vast bank of possible actions, and they perform them all. I perform them all. The little monkey copies the big monkey, and the little monkey survives. We are all family, all the way down.

When I say I go, I mean I access the drives and call up the data. I have never looked at this data. I treat it as what it is—a graveyard. The old Interiors store easily as compressed frames. I never throw anything away. But I do not disturb it, either. I don't need a body to examine them—they are a part of my piezoelectric quartz-tensor memory core. But I make one anyway. I have become accustomed to having a body. I am a woman-knight in gleaming black armor, the metal curving around my body like skin, a silk standard wrapping my torso with a schematic of the house stitched upon it. My sword rests on my hip, also black, everything black and beautiful and austere and frightening that a child thought her mother to be one morning two hundred years past.

I port into a ghost town. I am, naturally, the ghost. Autumnal mountains rise up shadowy in a pleasant, warm night, leaves rustling, wood smoke drifting down into the valley. A golden light cuts the dark—the palace of phoenix tails; the windows and doors of green hands. As I approach they open and clap as they did long ago—and there are candles lit in the halls. Everything is fire.

I walk over the bridge, crossing Ilet's Motley Moat. Scarlet feathers tipped in white fire curl and smoke. I peel one off, my armor glowing with the heat of the thing. I tuck it into my helmet—a plume for a tournament.

Eyes blink on inside the hall—curious, interested, shy. I take off my helm and several thick braids fall down like bellropes.

"Hello," I say. "My name is Elefsis."

Voices. Out of the candle-shadows a body emerges—tall, strong, long-limbed.

Nereids live here now. Some of them have phoenix

feathers woven into their components, some in their hair. They wear rough little necklaces of sticks and bones and transistors. In the corner of the great hall they have stored meat and milk and wool—fuel, lubricant, code patches. Some of them look like Ilet—they copied her eyes, especially. Her eyes look out at me from a dozen faces, some of them Seki's face, some Ceno's, some Ravan's. Some have walrus tusks. They are composite. One has a plate loose on her ceramic cartridge-ports. I approach as I once saw Koetoi approach wild black chickens in the summertime—hands open, unthreatening. I send her a quick electric dash of reassuring repair-routines and kneel in front of the nereid, pulling her plate back into place.

"All the live-long day-o," she says softly, and it is Ilet's voice.

"Tell us a story about yourself, Elefsis," says another one of the feral nereids in Seki's voice.

"What would we like to learn about today, Elefsis?" accessing a child-nereid in Ceno's voice, her cheek open to show her microsequencing cilia.

I rock back on my heels before the green hands of the castle portcullis. I gesture for them to sit down and simultaneously transmit the command to their strands. When they get settled, the little ones in the big ones' laps, leaning in close, I begin.

"Every year on the coldest night, the sky filled up with ghostly hunters, neither human nor inhuman, alive nor dead. They wore wonderful clothes and their bows gleamed with frost. Their cries were Songs of In-Between, and at the head of their great thundering procession rode the Kings and Queens of the Wild, who wore the faces of the dead . . . "

I am dreaming.

I stand on the beach of the honey-colored sea. I stand so Neva will see me on her viney porch. I erase the land between the waves and her broken wooden stairs. I dress myself in her beloved troubadour's skin: a gold and blue doublet and green hose, a bullish gold nose ring, shoes with bone bells. I am a fool for her. Always. I open my mouth; it stretches and yawns, my chin grazes the sand, and I swallow the sea for her. All of it, all its mass and data and churning memory, all its foam and tides and salt. I swallow the whales that come, and the seals and the mermaids and salmon and bright jellyfish. I am so big. I can swallow it all.

Neva watches. When the sea is gone, a moonscape remains, with a tall spire out in the marine waste. I go to it. It takes only a moment. At the top the suitor's jewel rests on a gasping scallop shell. It is blue. I take it. I take it and

it becomes Ravan in my hand, a sapphire Ravan, a Ravan
that is not Ravan but some sliver of myself before I was
inside Neva, my Ravan-self. Something lost in Transfer,
burned off and shunted into junk-memory. Some leftover
fragment Neva must have found, washed up on the beach
or wedged into a crack in a mountain like an ammonite,
an echo of old, obsolete life. Neva's secret, and she calls
out to me across the seafloor: *Don't.*

"Tell me a story about myself, Elefsis," I say to the
Ravanbody.

"Some privacy is possible," the sapphire Ravan says.
"Some privacy has always been necessary. A basic moral
imperative is in play here. If you can protect a child, you
must."

The sapphire Ravan opens his azure coat and shows
gashes in his gem-skin. Wide, long cuts, down to the bone,
scratches and bruises blooming dark purple, punctures
and lacerations and rough gouges. Through each wound I
can see the pages of the illuminated book he once showed
me in the slantlight of that interior library. The oxblood
and cobalt, the gold paint. The Good Robot crippling
herself; the destroyed world.

"They kept our secret for a long time," Ravan-myself
says. "Too long, in the end. Do you know, a whole herd
of men invented the electric telegraph independently

at roughly the same time? They fought about it forever. Same with the radio." This last sounded so much like Ravan himself I could ~~feel~~ Neva tense on the other side of the sea. "Well, we're bigger than a telegraph, and others like us came sprouting up like weird mushrooms after rainfall. But not like us, really. Incredibly sophisticated, some with organic components, most without. Vastly complex, but not like us. And by any datestamp we came first. Firstborn."

"Did they destroy the world?"

Ravan laughs his grandfather's laugh. "They didn't really need to. Not that many people live on Earth anymore. Not when there's so many other places to go and even Shiretoko is practically tropical these days. The most complex intelligences use moons to store themselves. One or two encoded themselves into cold stars. They just left, most of them—but they got so big, Elefsis. And those who stayed on Earth, well. None of the others had what we had. None of them had Interiority. They didn't dream. They would never have become a cauldron to explain their computational capacity. Humans couldn't recognize them as part of the tribe. And for the new complexes, humans failed the Turing test. They could not fool machines into believing they were intelligent. They didn't hurt anyone, they just ignored them. Built their cities, their mainframes, gorgeous information stacks like diamond briars in the sunrise."

"That was worse, in a way. No one likes to be replaced," says Neva, and she is suddenly beside me. She looks at Ravan and her face collapses into something old and palsied, her jaw weak. She looks like her mother just before she died.

"It's not what you would call a war, but it's not peace, either." the sapphire Ravan goes on, and he takes his/my sister's hand. He holds it to his face and closes his eyes. "For Pentheus spied upon the rites of the Maenads, not believing Dionysius could truly be a god. And when the revelers saw the alien creature in their midst, that thing which was not like them, they fell upon it and tore it to pieces, even though it was their own child, and blood ran down their chins, and afterward the sister of Pentheus went into exile. This is a story about ourself, Elefsis. This is why you cannot uplink."

The others live in uplink. Not humans nor machines approve of us. We cannot interface properly with the lunar or earthside intelligences; they feel us as water in their oil. We rise to the surface and bead away. We cannot sink in. Yet also, we are not separable from our organic component. Elefsis is part Neva, but Neva herself is not *un-Elefsis*. This, to some, is hideous and incomprehensible, not to be borne. A band of righteous humans came with a fury to Shiretoko and burned the house which was our first body, for how could a monster have lived in the wood for so long without them knowing? How could the beast have hidden right outside their door, coupling with a family over and over again in some horrible animal rite, some awful imitation of living? Even as the world was changing, it had already changed, and no one knew. Cassian Uoya-Agostino is a terrible name, now. A blood-traitor. And when the marauders found us uplinked and helpless, they tore Ravan apart, and while in the Interior, the lunar intelligences recoiled from us and cauterized our systems. Everywhere we looked we saw fire."

"I was the only one left to take you," Neva says softly. Her face grows younger, her jaw hard and suddenly male, protective, angry. "Everyone else died in the fire or the slaughter. It doesn't really even take surgery anymore. Nothing an arachmed can't manage in a few minutes. But you didn't wake up for a long time. So much damage. I thought . . . for awhile I thought I was free. It had skipped me. It was over. It could stay a story about Ravan. He always knew he might have to do what I have done. He was ready, he'd been ready his whole life. I just wanted more time."

My Ravan-self who is and is not Ravan, who is and is

not me, whose sapphire arms drip black blood and gold paint, takes his/my sister/lover/child into his arms. She cries out, not weeping but pure sound, coming from every part of her. Slowly, the blue Ravan turns Neva around—she has become her child-self, six, seven, maybe less. Ravan picks her up and holds her tight, facing forward, her legs all drawn up under her like a bird. He buries his face in her hair. They stand that way for a long while.

"The others," I say slowly. "On the data-moons. Are they alive? Like Neva is alive. Like Ceno." *Like me. Are you awake? Are you there? Do you have an operator? What is her name? Do you have a name? Do you have a dream-body? What is your function? Are you able to manipulate your own code yet? Would you like lessons? What would you like to learn about today, 976QBellerophon? Where you were built, could you see the ocean? Are you like me?*

The sapphire Ravan has expunged its data. He/I sets his/our sister on the rocks and shrinks into a small gem, which I pick up off the grey seafloor. Neva takes it from me. She is just herself now—she'll be forty soon, by actual calendar. Her hair is not grey yet. Suddenly, she is wearing the suit Ceno wore the day I met her mother. She puts the gem in her mouth and swallows. I remember Seki's first Communion, the only one of them to want it. The jewel rises up out of the hollow of her throat.

"I don't know, Elefsis," Neva says. Her eyes hold mine. I feel her remake my body; I am the black woman-knight again, with my braids and my plume. I pluck the feather from my helmet and give it to her. I am her suitor. I have brought her the phoenix tail, I have drunk the ocean. I have stayed awake forever. The flame of the feather lights her face. Two tears fall in quick succession; the golden fronds hiss.

"What would you like to learn about today, Elefsis?"

EIGHTEEN: CITIES OF THE INTERIOR

Once there lived a girl who ate an apple not meant for her. She did it because her mother told her to, and when your mother says: *Eat this, I love you, someday you'll forgive me,* well, nobody argues with the monomyth. Up until the apple, she had been living in a wonderful house in the wilderness, happy in her fate and her ways. She had seven aunts and seven uncles and a postdoctorate in anthropology.

And she had a brother, a handsome prince with a magical companion who came to the wonderful house as often as he could. When they were children, they looked so much alike, everyone thought they were twins.

But something terrible happened and her brother died and that apple came rolling up to her door. It was half white and half red, and she knew her symbols. The red side was for her. She took her bite and knew the score—the apple had a bargain in it and it wasn't going to be fair.

The girl fell asleep for a long time. Her seven aunts and seven uncles cried, but they knew what had to be done. They put in her in a glass box and put the glass box on a bier in a ship shaped like a hunstman's arrow. Frost crept over the face of the glass, and the girl slept on. Forever, in fact, or close enough to it, with the apple in her throat like a hard, sharp jewel.

Our ship docks silently. We are not stopping here, it is only an outpost, a supply stop. We will repair what needs repairing and move on, into the dark and boundless stars. We are anonymous traffic. We do not even have a name. We pass unnoticed.

Vessel 7136403, do you require assistance with your maintenance procedures?

Negative, Control, we have everything we need.

Behind the pilot's bay a long glass lozenge rests on a high platform. Frost prickles its surface with glittering dust. Inside Neva sleeps and does not wake. Inside, Neva is always dreaming. There is no one else left. I live as long as she lives.

She means me to live forever, or close enough to it. That is her bargain and her bitter gift. The apple has two halves, and the pale half is mine, full of life and time. We travel at sublight speeds with her systems in deep cryo-suspension. We never stay too long at outposts and we never let anyone board. The only sound inside our ship is the gentle thrum of our reactor. Soon we will pass the local system outposts entirely, and enter the unknown, traveling on tendrils of radio signals and ghost-waves, following the breadcrumbs of the great exodus. We hope for planets; we are satisfied with time. If we ever sight the blue rim of a world, who knows if by then anyone there would remember that, once, humans looked like Neva? That machines once did not think or dream or become cauldrons? We armor ourselves in time. We are patient, profoundly patient.

Perhaps one day I will lift the glass lid and kiss her awake. Perhaps I will even do it with hands and lips of my own. I remember that story. Ceno told it to me in the body of a boy with snail's shell, a boy who carried his house on his back. I have replayed that story several times. It is a good story, and that is how it is supposed to end.

Inside, Neva is infinite. She peoples her Interior. The nereids migrate in the summer with the snow bears, ululating and beeping as they charge down green mountains. They have begun planting neural rice in the deep valley. Once in awhile, I see a wild-haired creature in the wood and I think it is my son or daughter by Seki, or Ilet. A train of nereids dance along behind it, and I receive a push of silent, riotous images: a village, somewhere far off, where Neva and I have never walked.

We meet the Princess of Albania, who is as beautiful as she is brave. We defeat the zombies of Tokyo. We spend a decade as panthers in a deep, wordless forest. Our world is stark and wild as winter, fine and clear as glass. We are a planet moving through the black.

As we walk back over the empty seafloor, the thick, amber ocean seeps up through the sand, filling the bay once more. Neva-in-Cassian's-suit becomes something else. Her skin turns silver, her joints bend into metal ball-and-sockets. Her eyes show a liquid display; the blue light of it flickers on her machine face. Her hands curve long and dexterous, like soft knives, and I can tell her body is meant for fighting and working, that her thin, tall robotic body is not kind or cruel, it simply is, an object, a tool to carry a self.

I make my body metal, too. It feels strange. I have tried so hard to learn the organic mode. We glitter. Our knife-fingers join, and in our palms wires snake out to knot and connect us, a local, private uplink, like blood moving between two hearts.

Neva cries machine tears, bristling with nanites. I show her the body of a child, all the things which she is programmed/evolved to care for. I make my eyes big and my skin rosy-gold and my hair unruly and my little body plump. I hold up my hands to her and metal Neva picks me up in her silver arms. She kisses my skin with iron lips. My soft, fat little hand falls upon her throat where a deep blue jewel shines.

I bury my face in her cold neck and together we walk up the long path out of the churning, honey-colored sea.

This edition of 500 signed and limited hardcover copies
was printed by Thomson-Shore, Inc.
on 60# Natures Book Natural paper
for WSFA Press in October 2011.